When the Stars Form

When the Stars Form

Alexis Harris

RESOURCE *Publications* · Eugene, Oregon

WHEN THE STARS FORM

Resource Publications
An Imprint of Wipf and Stock Publishers
199 W. 8th Ave., Suite 3
Eugene, OR 97401

www.wipfandstock.com

PAPERBACK ISBN: 978-1-6667-3875-9
HARDCOVER ISBN: 978-1-6667-9982-8
EBOOK ISBN: 978-1-6667-9983-5

APRIL 18, 2022 9:54 AM

Dedicated to all my fans and loyal readers.
I appreciate your continued support,
and hope you've enjoyed The Star Chronicles!

Also, a special dedication to my pixie friend, Tabatha Hogueison.

Shout-outs to all my other friends and family
with characters named after them:
Kirstiana (Kirsten Stiles)
Lorena (Lauren Breed)
Shelbara (Shelby Bisgard)
Kendreil (Kendra Walters)
Morgalina (Morgan Harris)
Austinian (Austin Harris)
Sarafin (Sarah Carter)
Michaël (Michael Judah)
Dredon (Vondre Green)
Derekkian (Derrick Webb)

Contents

1	Vega	1
2	Kataran	11
3	Fughar	20
4	Garellis	31
5	Boreas	40
6	The Tree of Knowledge	48
7	Dirthix	56
8	Byun	66
9	Gachichken	75
10	Kiken	83
11	Thrindil	91
12	The Prophecy	98
13	Thaandor	109
14	Cabri	115
15	A New Keeper	126
16	The Oracle	133
17	A New Home	145
18	The End	152
	Pronunciation Guide	163
	Learn Dwarvish	164
	The Unsolvable Riddle	165
	Map	166

Vega

1

"Vega! Vega!" her mother shouted with worry, "Wake up!" She shook her daughter, tears streaming down her face. Finally, she called for her husband, "Dale! Hurry! She won't wake!"

Her father rushed into the room, dumping a bucket of cold water on her.

She gasped, sitting up and looking around the old, tired room of her family cottage. It was small and quaint, made from a gray wood. Her bedroom was tiny, her parents barely able to fit beside her twin bed. As she coughed and spit out the water that had gotten in her mouth, her parents embraced her gratefully. They were always worried about her when she had one of her "episodes."

"I'm fine, mom," Vega said as she was smothered. Her quilt was soaked now, and she was beginning to shiver.

"Get her some dry clothes and bedding, Lenore," her father said, "I'll get a fire going." He was a tall, burly man with a ragged blonde beard and brown eyes.

Her mother—a plump woman with brown hair and eyes—reluctantly hurried from the room.

Vega was a young girl near the age of ten. She had brown eyes, and her hair was a mixture of gold and amber. She looked up at her father as he lifted her out of her bed, carrying her through the cottage to the family room, and setting her on the armchair beside the fireplace. He hurriedly got a fire going as shivers began to rack her body.

It wasn't long before Lenore arrived with dry clothes, helping her daughter change quickly. She wrapped her in a dry quilt, scooting her closer to the blaze. "It's going to be alright, sweetheart," she said, pushing her wet hair out of her face.

Vega couldn't do much besides nod as she shivered, trying to get warm.

"What are we going to do, Dale?" Lenore said, leaning into her husband's chest.

He wrapped his arms around her, kissing her forehead, "We'll figure something out."

"Wh-what's wr-wrong with me-e?" Vega asked, looking forlornly up at her parents.

"Nothing, sweetheart," her mother said, embracing her around the thick quilt, "You're perfect."

Despite what her mother told her, she knew there was more to what was happening with her, and it scared her. This was the eighth time this had happened in the last month, and the doctors could provide them no answers. She wasn't sure exactly what went on when she blacked out, but from what she overheard, her eyes would roll to the back of her head, and she would become unresponsive. She never remembered anything except waking up to a bucket of cold water being tossed over her. Then, she would get a painful headache, which would last a few hours.

"I'll make you some hot tea," Lenore said, hurrying from the room.

Dale pulled up a chair, sitting beside her, "Do you remember anything this time?"

Vega shook her head.

He sighed, "We've already called upon every doctor in the area. I'm not sure what else we can do."

"It's alright, father," she said as she warmed up, "I'm okay."

He looked away. Finally, when her mother returned with the tea, he got up, heading out of the room.

"Here," she said, "Drink this."

She took the cup, sipping the hot liquid, and allowing it to warm her body.

Lenore watched her worriedly. She tried to hide it, but it showed.

When everything had calmed down, her mother took her back to her room. Her father had changed the bedding for her, and she tucked her in to sleep. "Goodnight, my child," she said lovingly, kissing her forehead, "Pleasant dreams."

Once her mother had left the room, Vega closed her eyes, letting herself drift off.

When she awoke, her headache was faint, but still lingering. She climbed out of bed, slowly making her way to the family room. When she opened the door, she saw that her parents were packing. "What's going on?" she asked.

"Vega, sweetie, you're awake," Lenore said, looking at her in surprise.

Dale looked up from packing long enough to say, "Get your things. We're leaving in an hour."

Vega looked back and forth between her parents in confusion, "Where are we going?"

Her mother crossed over to her, gently pulling her to where they were filling bags with clothes, food, and supplies, "We're going to the village of Kataran in Katangalo. It's rumored there's a medicine man there who can help you."

"We're leaving Millhaymae?" she asked, looking around her childhood home.

"Yes," her father said, "There's no one here who can help us. Do you want to keep having episodes?"

She shook her head.

"Go get dressed, sweetheart," her mother said, "And grab anything you need to take with you."

Vega stood there, unmoving. She couldn't believe they were leaving home. She was frozen in place.

"Now," her father said sternly, "We have to go."

Finally, she turned, heading back to her room. She looked around at the tiny wardrobe and bed, the faded pink quilt, and all her dolls and stuffed animals. She got dressed slowly, and then let a few tears stream down as she chose the outfits and toys she would take with her, and which ones would be left behind.

Eventually, Lenore came in, bringing her bag with her, so they could put her things inside. When she saw her daughter standing there, staring sadly at her toys, she said, "You would have parted with them eventually, darling. You're getting older now. I know it seems hard, but one day, you won't even remember them. You'll be happier getting the help you need than saving all your dolls."

Vega looked down, squeezing her favorite doll tightly.

"Come on, sweetheart," she said softly, "It's time to go."

She put her toys and clothes in the bag her mother had brought, and took her hand. They walked out of her room together, saying goodbye to their home.

Dale was waiting outside, and he hurried to grab their bags when he saw them coming out. He had their wagon ready to go; the horses hitched to the front of it. He loaded the bags, and then helped the two of them get on. When they were all situated, he got the horses going, and they rode off toward Katangalo.

They rode through the land of Millhaymae, avoiding the areas commonly patrolled by slave traders. Dale was ever ready to protect his family if needed. His rough, blonde beard looked yellow in the sunlight. Lenore hugged her daughter tightly, trying to hide her anxiety. Her brown locks kept falling out of her bonnet, but she brushed them away.

Vega wasn't sure what her new life would hold, or if they would ever return home. But, she was hopeful that someone could finally help her. She'd seen every doctor in their area, and no one seemed to be able to help. Her episodes had gotten more frequent lately, and she knew her parents were worried. She clutched her doll tightly as they rode through the forests of her homeland.

It took them a few days to reach the border of Katangalo, stopping in a couple of villages along the way. The further they got from home, the more anxious Vega grew. She stared at her reflection in the water of the river, her brown eyes wide. Her golden and amber hair fell around her, tangled.

Finally, they could see the circular huts of the village of Kataran over a hill. Vega sat up straight, straining to see. She was as curious as she was nervous. Her mother pulled her into her lap so she could see better, and her father shook the reins, getting the horses to quicken their pace.

When the villagers spotted them riding in, they gathered nosily in the square. Dale pulled their wagon to a stop, hopping down. Lenore held her daughter close to her chest, looking around at the curious faces around them.

After a few moments, a handful of elders came forward, parting the crowd. One of them held up his arms, silencing them. "Welcome," he said, "What brings you to our village?"

Dale looked at each of them carefully, "We have come seeking a visit with your medicine man. We've heard tell that he can help our daughter."

Everyone stared at Vega, then.

"What's the nature of her condition?" he asked.

"It's nothing contagious," he replied guardedly, looking around, "But, if you wouldn't mind, I'd rather not share the details with the entire village."

The elder nodded, beckoning them, "Come with me."

Another elder offered to take their wagon and horses to the inn for them, so Lenore climbed out of the wagon, helping Vega down as well. The three of them followed the first elder, making their way through the village and to a small hut on the outskirts, near the forest. He gestured for them to follow him inside, and they entered the tiny hut.

It was decorated in red and orange, with tapestries along the walls. There were four beds inside, one of them occupied. A strange old man with a scraggly beard and an orange robe was standing over the person in the bed, waving an object which produced smoke. He was skinny enough to see his bones. The person lying down was coughing as the smoke entered his lungs. It smelled of sage and lavender.

He didn't seem to notice anyone had entered his hut, as he chanted over the sick person, continuing to wave the smoke over him. Finally, he finished his chants, setting the object that produced the smoke on a nearby table. "To what do I owe the pleasure, Elder Khantis?" he asked.

"This couple has traveled a great distance seeking your aid for their daughter," he replied.

He looked at Vega then, studying her. After a long pause, he said, "What seems to be the problem?"

Dale cleared his throat, saying, "She has these episodes, where she goes stiff, her eyes roll back in her head, and she becomes unresponsive."

"She doesn't remember what happened after," Lenore added, "And she gets bad headaches when she wakes."

"We have to wake her with a bucket of cold water," her father continued, "There's nothing else that will snap her out of it."

"They're getting worse, too, of late," her mother said, "They've been occurring more frequently. None of the doctors in our area know what's wrong with her." She looked at him pleadingly, "Please help us. We don't know what to do."

He nodded, "I can help you." As her parents embraced, full of joy and relief, he said, "You will need to stay here for observation until her next episode. Don't wake her. Just come get me."

Elder Khantis cleared his throat, "Thank you, Fughar." He waved his arm to the three of them, then, "We shall offer you a place in our inn until the observation is complete."

Her father nodded, and they followed Elder Khantis to the inn. Their wagon and horses were waiting for them, and they were given a room. It had a large enough bed for the three of them to share. It had faded yellow bedding, a small wardrobe, and an end table.

"Lenore, why don't you take Vega and wash up," Dale said, "I'll see about getting us some food."

She nodded, escorting their daughter to the washroom, and helping her get clean. Vega had so many thoughts running through her head as she sat in the tub. She was scared and hopeful at the same time for what Fughar might be able to do for her. Could he really make her better? She was ready to find out.

"Hi, I'm Cassie," a young girl said, approaching Vega. She had curly, brown hair and gray eyes.

"I'm Vega," she replied shyly.

"You wanna play?" she asked.

Vega looked back at her parents uncertainly. They nodded, her mother saying, "Just be sure to be back in time for dinner."

She smiled, happy to have at least a little bit of freedom to be a kid. They were stuck in this town at the inn until she had another episode, so the medicine man could observe her, and determine how to help her. In the meantime, they had nothing to occupy their time.

As soon as she'd gotten permission, Cassie said, "Come on!" and the two girls took off running. There were several other kids from around the village that ran up to join them. They led Vega to the side of the town square where they had lines drawn in the dirt. They had several games they were playing, and Cassie showed her how to hopscotch.

She'd never really gotten to play with other children before. Most of her childhood had been spent at home, with a never-ending parade of doctors. She smiled at the sight of so many games to play, and so many children to play with.

When they got bored with hopscotch, she joined a game of kickball. She'd never gotten to play any of those games before. It didn't take her long to catch on, though, as she watched the other kids go first. Running around the bases gave her a sense of elation. The other kids cheered her on as she ran, cheering even louder when she made it to the base.

Vega barely noticed when it got dark, until the other kids started getting called home for dinner. Finally, she said *goodbye* to her new friend, Cassie, and made her way back to the inn. She was just in time, as her parents were waiting in the restaurant on the main floor of the inn so they could eat.

"Did you have fun today?" her mother asked, smiling.

"Yes," she replied, "We played hopscotch and kickball, and all kinds of games!"

Lenore smiled lovingly at her daughter, "That's wonderful, dear."

"Are you feeling alright?" her father asked, "No headaches? You didn't have an episode?"

"I feel fine," Vega replied, "In fact, I feel great."

"I'm glad," her mother said, eyeing her father, "You deserve to just be a kid."

Dale looked at her, "Yes, you do. I just hope this medicine man can finally give you that opportunity."

Vega nodded, eating her meal of roast beef and potatoes. She knew both of her parents wanted the best for her, but she wasn't sure if she'd ever get it. Though they were both happy to see her being a kid, they were also both still worried about her. They tried to hide it, but she could tell. *Well, Fughar, let's see what you can do,* she thought.

With none of them sure when her next episode would be, her father decided to establish a more permanent arrangement for them. He went to petition the village council for a small plot of land, and to gain residency in their village.

In the meantime, her mother spent the day chatting with the other mothers of the village, trying to get in with the locals to increase their chances of gaining residency. Vega found Cassie again, and the two girls spent the day exploring in the nearby forest.

"We can search for pretty rocks," Cassie said, as they moved through the vibrant green trees.

Vega simply nodded, watching her new friend clamber through the grass to find shiny stones. She wasn't sure what the point of collecting rocks was, but she wasn't about to question someone willing to offer their friendship. They found many varieties of stones she deemed beautiful, and she wrapped them in her apron to take home. Vega helped by pointing out any she spotted, allowing Cassie to decide their worth.

The forest was beautiful. She stared at the golden sunlight that penetrated the green leaves. Small forest animals rustled through the brush, going about their everyday lives. There were squirrels, rabbits, and foxes. She spotted a couple of deer as well, but they took off when they saw the girls, full of fear. Birds chirped overhead, and she was happy to be in a place so full of life.

When Cassie's apron was full, they headed back to the village. She rattled on and on about her rock collection the whole way. Vega listened, smiling. She didn't mind all of her talking. In fact, it was nice, just hearing about normal things.

"Vega!" Lenore shouted, "Where have you been?"

"We were just—" she began.

"Get over here right now!" she yelled.

Vega hung her head, embarrassed, as she walked over to her mother.

"Uh, I'll see you later," Cassie said, scurrying off.

"You can't just wander off," her mother said, "We had no idea where you were. What if you had another episode?"

Vega remained silent, staring at the ground.

Lenore sighed, softening her tone, "From now on, only play in the square, okay?"

She nodded.

"Come on; it's time for dinner."

When Vega was tucked into bed, trying to sleep, her parents began whispering. They obviously thought she'd already drifted off. So, she remained silent, listening.

"How'd it go today?" Lenore asked.

Dale sighed, "They said they need to make sure their medicine man can help us before they grant us permanent residency. They don't want to say yes, only for us to move again if it doesn't work out."

It was her turn to sigh. After a pause, she said, "It does make sense. But, what can we do? We can't afford to stay here until we know."

"They agreed to cover our stay at their inn until we have an answer. Then, if he can help us, they will consider granting us permanent residency. And if not, we're free to go."

She sighed again, this time with relief, "That's wonderful news."

"Yes," he agreed, "They've been very generous and hospitable."

"So, now we wait," she said.

"That's all we *can* do," he agreed.

Vega almost *wanted* an episode to happen, now. She wanted to get the help she needed, and she didn't want her parents to lose all their money waiting on a cure. Each day they spent waiting for an episode seemed an eternity. Before, it seemed like they happened too often. Now that they wanted one to happen, they were refusing to flare up.

But, in the meantime, she was enjoying the opportunity to play with the village kids. Unfortunately, she wasn't allowed to go to the woods with Cassie, but they could still play in the square. She even brought her to her family's hut to show her her complete rock collection. It filled the back of her bedroom wall-to-wall, leaving a path between it and her bed. Though she still didn't understand the purpose, she had to admit her dedication was impressive.

"I wish you could come to the forest with me," she said.

"Me, too," Vega agreed, "It was nice."

"Why won't your mom let you go?" Cassie asked.

"She doesn't want me to get hurt."

She laughed, "All kids get hurt. It's what we do. You can't prevent that."

Vega smiled, "Try telling her that."

Cassie sighed, "Well, we can still play hopscotch, I suppose."

She nodded.

They made their way out of her hut, and she turned around, holding out her hand, "Come on. Let's go play."

Vega took her hand, and they started to skip toward the square. Suddenly, she felt strange, and she saw flashes of Cassie getting attacked by a boy in the village. Then, everything went black.

Kataran

2

She wasn't sure how long she was out, but she heard bits and pieces of conversation.

"Vega!" her mother shouted in panic.

"Someone get Fughar!" Elder Khantis said.

She felt her father carrying her. Then, she faded to the blackness again.

She could hear Fughar's voice, "We must not wake her."

"What?" her father yelled, "Are you crazy?"

"Did the other doctors heal her?" he asked calmly. When there was no response, he said, "We must wait and ride it out until she wakes on her own." After another pause, he asked, "How old is she?"

"Almost ten," her mother replied.

Blackness took her again, and she was standing in the forest. There was a beautiful stone on the ground. As she watched, Cassie appeared, happily picking up the stone and putting it in her apron. She was alone. Vega felt bad she couldn't join her. Then, she saw the boy from the village she'd seen before. He was older than them—probably around fifteen. He had a dark gleam in his eyes. He snuck up behind her. While she was bent over picking up a rock, he jumped out, wrapping his arms around her and dragging her behind a tree.

She couldn't watch the rest, turning away in horror, and trying to block out the sounds. Cassie's screams echoed through her mind as she came back into consciousness. Vega screamed, sitting up, and looking around the red-and-orange-garbed hut of the medicine man.

"It's alright," Fughar said, holding her, "You're here, now."

Her parents stared worriedly at her, holding each other.

"Bring me a glass of water for her," he said.

Her mother did as he said, rushing it to her daughter.

Fughar waited until she drank it. When she had calmed down, he asked, "What did you see?"

Vega looked at him.

"We told you, she doesn't remember anything," Lenore said.

"I asked Vega," he replied, focused on her, "What did you see?"

Tears began streaming down as she said, "I saw Cassie. A boy attacked her in the forest."

Everyone's eyes widened as they looked at her. Finally, Fughar asked, "Did you recognize this boy?"

She nodded.

"Do you know his name?"

Vega shook her head.

"Could you point him out if you saw him?"

She tried to wipe her tears away as they kept coming, and she was barely able to answer, "Yes."

He nodded, "Come with me."

Despite her parents' protests, she accompanied Fughar into the square where the kids were playing, and she saw him. He was tall and scrawny, with brown hair and eyes. Vega raised a trembling finger and pointed at him.

"Thank you," he said. When she'd lowered her hand, he shouted, "Billy!"

The boy turned toward them, then. Vega backed up into her parents.

"Take her back to the hut," Fughar said, "I shall return shortly."

As her parents dragged her back to his hut, she watched him lead Billy toward Town Hall, where the Council of Elders assemble. She wasn't sure what was happening, but she hoped she could trust Fughar.

When he returned to the hut, Elder Khantis was with him.

"What's all this, then?" he asked, looking at Vega.

"It's alright," Fughar said, "Tell him what you saw."

She repeated her story to Elder Khantis, telling him what had happened.

He stared at her skeptically, "What proof have you that she can see the future?"

See the future? she thought in wonder.

"I've seen episodes like hers before," Fughar said, "It was a vision."

"Vision?" Lenore asked in confusion.

"Our daughter's no psychic," Dale added.

"Enough of this nonsense," Elder Khantis snapped.

Fughar's eyes turned dark, "You would condemn one of our own to such a fate?"

He sighed, "I cannot be expected to convict someone of a crime they haven't committed. It's not enough that she says he's going to."

"So we must wait until it actually happens to do anything about it?" he yelled.

"I'm afraid we have no choice," Elder Khantis replied, "We have no evidence against him. We have no proof her 'visions' are real and accurate." He was silent a moment, before walking out of the hut.

There was a long pause before Fughar said, "I'm sorry. I put too much faith in our council. They do not believe your vision."

Vega was overwhelmed for a moment, knowing the images that had disturbed her so vividly were actually going to happen, and no one would do anything to stop them. *Cassie,* she thought, tears forming in her eyes.

"Vega?" her mother said softly, touching her shoulder.

"No!" she yelled, shaking her off and running from the hut. She couldn't take the knowledge that her "episodes" were actually visions, and that nobody but Fughar took them seriously enough to try to prevent the atrocity she'd seen. That there was nothing she could do to save her friend.

Her tears flowed freely, and she looked off into the square. Cassie wasn't playing with the other kids. As she surveyed the town in a panic, she caught sight of Billy, wandering into the forest. Her breath caught, and her eyes widened as she realized her vision was about to come true. *No,* she thought, *I won't stand idly by. My mother may have forbidden me to play in the forest, but I'm not playing.*

With that, she gritted her teeth, determined, and snuck past Cassie's hut. She noticed a few dirty dishes sitting outside. They were all from travel, including canteens, bowls, and a frying pan. She snatched the pan, hurrying into the woods, and sneaking behind the trees.

When she caught sight of Billy again, she followed him, staying out of sight. It didn't take long before Cassie came into view. She was bent over, picking up some stones. As much as she didn't want anything to happen to her friend, she knew she had to wait until he grabbed her, so she could prove her vision was true.

As she watched, he snuck up behind her and grabbed her, starting to drag her behind the tree. Vega used the momentary distraction, running out from her hiding place and swinging the frying pan. She hit him in the head, knocking him out.

Cassie scrambled out from under his unconscious body, tears of panic streaming from her eyes. She looked up at her savior, gray eyes growing wide, "Vega?"

She let go of the pan, dropping to her knees. Her whole body shook as it tried to comprehend its own adrenaline.

Cassie crawled over, hugging her, "Oh, Vega, thank you."

She hugged her friend, the two girls crying for a moment from a combination of fear, adrenaline, and relief.

Finally, Cassie said, "I thought you weren't allowed to play in the woods. Plus, you were in the medicine man's hut after you passed out." She shot her a confused look.

Vega raised her brown eyes to look at her, "Fughar figured out what my episodes are. They're visions. I can see the future."

Her eyes widened again, "See the future?"

She nodded, quietly adding, "I saw what was going to happen to you."

Her eyes somehow grew even wider, practically bulging out of her head. After a pause, she looked down at the unconscious Billy, a couple of brown curls falling in her face.

"I'm *not* allowed in the forest," Vega added, "But the elders refused to listen. I had to do *something*. I couldn't just let that happen to you." She let a few more tears stream down as she thought of what she'd seen again.

Cassie reached out, brushing Vega's golden and amber hair out of her face. "Thank you," she said, "You're a true friend."

The two girls got up, dragging Billy out of the forest. He regained consciousness at one point along their return journey, and they had to knock him out again, Cassie taking the honor this time. Finally, they reached the square, and everyone stopped and stared as they dragged him to Town Hall.

When they entered, they dragged him before the elders, who were all staring, wide-eyed. "What happened?" Elder Khantis asked.

Vega smirked, shaking her head at him in disgust at his inaction.

"He attacked me in the forest," Cassie said, "Vega here saved me by hitting him over the head with a frying pan. If not for her, I'm not sure what would have happened, but it would have been a lot worse."

He swallowed, looking at each of them. Finally, he cleared his throat, saying, "Elder Danvers, fetch the sheriff."

The elder nodded, scurrying from the room. The two girls looked at each other, relieved. Elder Danvers didn't take long, bringing the sheriff within a few minutes. As Billy regained consciousness, shackles were placed upon his wrists, and he was placed under arrest. He stared at them, dazed and confused, as he was dragged from the room.

Over the next couple of weeks, Vega felt freer than she ever had. She could be herself, she could be normal, she could play with her new friends. She now understood what her episodes were, and how to handle them. The village council granted her and her family residency, and her father got to work building them a hut. Her mother planted seeds to grow some crops, so they could contribute to the village's income. And, Vega was able to start school. For most kids, it was a drag. But, for her, it was wonderful. She was finally able to be normal. She could join the other kids her age and *learn*. Moving to Kataran seemed to be the best thing that had ever happened to her.

"Everyone, we have a new student in our midst," Miss Geneva said, waving her arm toward Vega, "Please make her feel welcome." She was a young teacher with blonde hair and green eyes.

As Vega uncertainly scanned the room, looking for a seat, she made eye contact with Cassie. She smiled, eagerly pointing at the seat next to her, which was vacant. She made her way over, taking the seat.

"Now, what do you guys know about the elves?" Miss Geneva asked.

A little boy raised his hand.

She nodded to him, "Yes, Duncan."

"We're not supposed to talk about things that don't pertain to our village. We're here to learn about farming, combat, math, language, and markets."

She straightened, blinking. After a pause, she said, "Yes, well, I feel it would be beneficial to learn about things beyond the human realm."

"What for?" another kid asked.

"If you're traveling, and you come across an elf or a dwarf, don't you want to know how to act?" she said, "Besides, don't you find the world around us to be more interesting than farming and math?"

"Not really," Duncan said.

Miss Geneva sighed, "Well, I do. Now, do any of you know anything about elves?"

Everyone was quiet, no one raising their hand.

"Nobody?" she asked, disappointed. After another pause, she said, "Very well. Today, we will learn about the customs of the elves. First off, they are a very formal race . . . "

Vega was fascinated to learn about any subject, but the other children of the village tuned their teacher out as she explained the mannerisms and traditions of the elves. She wondered why none of them seemed keen to learn. They were all either sleeping, chatting, or throwing folded pieces of paper around the room. She began to see that school wasn't all it was cracked up to be. That maybe, being unusual was a good thing.

"Psst, hey," Cassie whispered.

She turned to look at her friend.

"Are you interested in really learning this stuff?"

Vega looked at her in confusion, nodding.

"Miss Geneva hosts a private session after school for kids who actually want to learn. She tries in class, but the elders won't hear of her education plan. They don't care about scholastics. They only care about preparing us kids for life in this village. By tomorrow, she'll be back to the usual subjects. Just wait and see. But, if you want to really learn, stay here after the other kids leave."

When the class cleared out, Vega remained seated beside Cassie. There were only two other kids besides them who stayed behind. When Miss Geneva turned around, she was smiling, "Vega, I'm so pleased to see you're an avid learner."

She nodded shyly, unsure what to say.

"Have you studied other cultures before?"

She shook her head.

Miss Geneva cleared her throat, "Well, since you're new, I would love to have you take an assessment to determine what knowledge you already have."

"I've . . . never been to school before," Vega replied nervously.

Everyone stared at her in surprise. She could feel their eyes boring into her.

"Never been to school?" she asked softly.

"My parents were worried about my episodes," she said quietly.

She nodded. After a pause, she said, "Well . . . I have a lot to teach you then, haven't I?"

Vega smiled.

"Let's begin with what we were discussing in class today: elves. Now, what can you all tell me about them?"

The other kids raised their hands, one explaining their natural preferences, such as living in the forest, forming the trees into their cities, and their plant-based diet. Another explained their innate magic, due to being an ancient species, and how over half of them could wield magic—more than any other species—using it for everyday purposes, even to build their cities. He also explained how they age at a much slower rate than humans, living four times as long. Cassie explained their formal, graceful, slow-moving, and peaceful nature, as well as their sharp senses and quick reflexes.

Vega sat listening, in awe over the elegance of these creatures known as elves. She was also a bit intimidated, seeing how much her peers knew compared to her. Nine years with no formal schooling had put her behind the curve.

"Very good, everyone," Miss Geneva said, "I'm impressed." After a pause, she said, "Vega, why don't you and I work together today, so I can start catching you up on the basics?"

She nodded.

"The rest of you, we'll pick up tomorrow with a lesson in elven history."

The three of them left, and Miss Geneva spent the afternoon working with Vega on her math, language, and village history. When dinner-time rolled around, she dismissed her. Her parents had been wondering where she'd been, but when she explained, they were happy the teacher was willing to work with her after school to catch her up to the other kids.

The next day, as Cassie had predicted, Miss Geneva stuck to the basic subjects, much to Vega's disappointment. "Why does the village frown on scholastic achievement?" she asked Cassie when class had ended.

"They think it's a waste of time. We're a farming village. That's our life. They don't see a point in learning anything else when we don't need it to farm."

After a pause, she asked, "Then, why do *you* want to learn?"

She looked at her, then, "I don't want to live my life in ignorance of the world around me. There's more to life than farming. There's so much to learn and do and be. I think it's a terrible waste of a good mind to shut out learning."

Vega smiled, "I couldn't agree more."

The following day, they learned about the dwarves in their after-school session. The other three talked about how they were short, but with the complex of a giant. They build huge, magnificent structures, preferring to tunnel into the earth to do so. They are extremely prideful creatures, sensitive to insult. They enjoy manual labor jobs, happy to use their hands, and maintain their strength. They can come across as rough around the edges, but the majority of them have good hearts. They're family-oriented. They enjoy parties; singing, dancing, drinking, and smoking. Their diet consists of meats and cheeses, and they pride themselves on their unique cooking methods, bringing out the flavors of both. They tend to be much more hospitable to outsiders than their counterparts, the elves. They live by their code of honor, and would rather die than be dishonorable.

They learned about dragons and dragon riders, how they came to form bonds with dragons, and what that bond entails. They learned how riders are chosen from amongst humans and elves, and how the land they created is a fusion of cultures thanks to this.

They learned about wizards, and how humans and elves can be born with the ability to wield magic. Since there are so many elves with this ability, they don't feel the need to leave home. But, the human wizards created their own realm to live together in peace. They chose to be in close proximity to the dragon riders, since riders are also able to wield magic, due to their dragons. The tough part was when a pair of wizards or riders had a non-magical child. Their child could not stay in their realm. So, as people from all over migrated to the wizard and dragon rider realms if they were able to wield magic, or if they were joining a class to become a rider, so non-magical beings had to leave. Vega imagined that would be extremely difficult, to say goodbye.

They also learned about magical creatures. There were so many of them, she knew it would take a long time to cover. They learned of the elemental birds: dirthens, dwervas, auristras, and phoenixes. They learned of siladines and trolls, which dwelt in the land of the dwarves, along with the dirthens. They enjoy the dwarven caves, preferring to live underground.

They also learned of all the incredible creatures that dwelt in the land of the elves: mermaids, pixies, stags, nymphs, unicorns, and more, along with the dwervas and auristras. The ancient, magical forests of Gliken were the natural habitat of these creatures. It was the one place they felt safe. Vega felt like she could relate to them, needing a familiar place to feel safe in this confusing world.

They even covered the darker creatures of the world, which dwelt in the land of Kogatsa. There were vekkens, the evil counterparts of dragons; faeries, the darker version of nymphs; and kodrizans, creatures made by dark magic and ritual sacrifice. Dark wizards would create entire armies of them, killing hundreds of innocents to do so. They were the product of death and malice.

She also continued to work with Miss Geneva individually, catching herself up on the all-important subjects of grammar, spelling, writing, reading, and math. She was happy, finally being able to learn. She hadn't had an episode since she'd saved Cassie, and she was elated, finally able to start feeling normal.

Her parents even seemed to be relaxing—not hovering as much, and not worrying as much. Her father finished building the house, and her mother got their field of crops ready to grow. They finally had a home, and one she could feel comfortable and be herself in. She was glad that they left Millhaymae. Though it was hard at first, it had all been worth it.

Fughar

3

"Miss . . . Geneva, is it?" a man with brown hair and brown eyes asked, entering the schoolhouse.

She looked up from what she was writing, "May I help you?"

"Yeah," he said, "You can stop putting ideas in my Matthew's head."

"I beg your pardon?" she said, rising from behind her desk.

"You heard me," he said, staring at her, "These after-school 'sessions' need to stop. If it ain't fit for school, it ain't fit to be teachin'."

Miss Geneva looked at him steadily, "I don't force anyone to attend. If they want to stay behind, and they show a desire to learn, I'm willing to teach them. Matthew's a bright boy. He has so much potential."

"He has the potential to take over my farm one day!" he shouted, "He don't need to learn nothin' about no elves and dwarves and all that other bullshit! How is that gonna help him sow, or plow, or harvest crops? The village council already told you not to be teachin' that stuff! I better not hear of my boy stayin' behind no more!"

"Is that a threat, Mr. Hayward?" she asked, standing her ground.

He walked up to her, "Take it how you wanna take it."

"I'm doing nothing wrong," she said, "I'm here to teach, and I'm teaching. I follow the prescribed curriculum during school hours. And, I don't respond well to idle threats."

"Idle threats?" he said, looking at her questioningly. Suddenly, he slapped her, shouting, "I'll show you idle!" While she was hunched over, clutching at her face, he grabbed her by her apron string, throwing her into the wall.

Blood trickled from the top of her head, and she clutched her hair, looking up at him.

"No more private lessons," he said. With that, he kicked her in the face, striding out of the schoolhouse.

Miss Geneva lay on the ground, blood flowing around her from her head, nose, and mouth.

"No!" Vega yelled, sitting up. She looked around the darkened bedroom. It resembled her room back home. Her father had modeled their house after the one in Millhaymae. She felt sweat sticking to her everywhere. It had been months since she'd had an episode. Now that she knew what they were, they still scared her. In fact, they scared her even more. She climbed out of bed, going to the kitchen to get a drink and clear her head.

She wasn't sure what to do with the information, now. She almost preferred when her father would wake her with a bucket of cold water before she could see anything. Now, she'd seen two haunting visions. She'd been able to prevent the first one, but she wasn't so sure about the second.

When morning came, Vega headed to Town Hall, telling the Council of Elders about her vision. Once again, her claim was ignored. She'd thought that after the last time, they'd listen. But, Elder Khantis was stubborn. He insisted no action could be taken against someone for a crime they hadn't yet committed.

With no help from them, she went to Miss Geneva. Since it was the weekend, and they didn't have school, she had to go to her hut. She walked through the dirt streets of town, knocking on her door.

She answered, looking at her curiously, "Vega? What are you doing here?"

"Hi, Miss Geneva," she said, "Can I talk to you for a minute?"

"Sure," she said, stepping to the side to let her enter her hut, "Do your parents know you're here?"

Her hut was lively, full of beautiful art and colorful decorations. Vega took a seat on her pink couch, looking at the black-and-white-striped vase on the table before it.

Miss Geneva sat across from her on her blue chair, "What did you want to talk to me about?"

"Do you know about me?" she asked, "About my condition?"

She nodded, "Yes. As your teacher, your parents informed me, in case you have an episode during school, so I'd know what to do."

"Do you know what my episodes are?"

"Fughar told them they're visions—that you see the future."

Vega nodded, "I had a vision last night . . . a vision about you."

Miss Geneva looked at her in surprise, blonde locks falling in her face.

"I tried to tell the Council of Elders, but they wouldn't listen," she said hopelessly.

Her teacher stared at her silently, green eyes full of confusion.

Vega sighed, "I saw you get attacked . . . by Mr. Hayward—Matthew's father."

She gasped, eyes widening.

"He was angry about the after-school lessons, and he was yelling at you about them. You stood your ground, and then he . . . he slapped you, and threw you into the wall, and kicked your face," she said, tears forming in her eyes, "They may not have believed me, but you have to! You have to take precautions to defend yourself!"

Miss Geneva looked horrified, "I believe you, Vega. Thank you for telling me."

"Then . . . you'll be careful?"

She nodded, "I will. Now, you'd better get going before your parents start wondering where you are."

The next day, after their after-school session, Vega stuck around, hiding alongside the schoolhouse. She waited, but nobody came. The next few days, she continued to wait around, but nobody came to the school. Over a week went by, and she was starting to think no one would ever come.

Then, finally, one day she saw Mr. Hayward approaching the schoolhouse. She watched through the window as he entered, surprising Miss

Geneva. When he began yelling, she clutched the bat she'd brought with her, preparing to jump in and save her teacher. She took a deep breath, hurrying to the door.

When she looked inside, she saw a sight quite different from her vision. Miss Geneva was standing there, holding a sword, which was pointed right at Mr. Hayward. He had his hands up in surprise, "Alright, I'm goin'. But, don't think I won't report this to the Council of Elders."

She was silent, holding the sword steadily.

Matthew's father turned around, storming out of the schoolhouse.

Vega slowly came around the building and through the door, dragging the bat beside her.

Miss Geneva looked up, "Vega?" After a pause, she sheathed the sword, running over and hugging her.

"I wanted to make sure my vision didn't come true," she said, "But, it looks like you didn't need my help."

"I told you I'd be careful," she replied, "But, thank you for your concern."

"If you saw what I'd seen, you'd be concerned, too," she said.

Miss Geneva smiled, "Get home. Your parents will be worried."

Vega nodded, heading back home for dinner.

When the weekend came, so did Vega's tenth birthday. Her parents hosted a party at their hut, inviting many of the villagers. Cassie, Matthew, and Marcus attended—the other kids from their after-school sessions with Miss Geneva. The four of them had become fast friends due to their shared love of learning.

They laid out tables and chairs, and served all kinds of desserts, from pies to puddings. She and the other kids ran around, playing all the usual games, and eating the delicious array of food. Vega had never had a real birthday party before, where she could celebrate with other kids her age. She felt her grin would be permanent, as the wind blew through her hair while she was running between tables with Cassie as the boys tried to tag them.

"Run, Vega!" Cassie shouted, brushing past her. When their skin touched, she felt a shiver run through her, and she blacked out.

She saw Cassie, looking thin and frail. Her lips were dry, and her voice was raspy, "Mother says we're moving. I'm sorry, Vega. I'll miss you." After a long pause, she said, "It's this drought. We're not the only ones leaving.

The village is done for. We have no food and no water. We're dead if we stay. We all are."

She came back into awareness, thinking, *No. This village has become my home. It's the only place I've ever felt free to be myself. They have to listen to me this time . . .*

"Vega!" her mother was hovering over her worriedly.

"Mother," she said, "I had a vision. I need to talk with the Council of Elders. And I need Fughar's help."

"For now, let's get you some food and drink, and some rest."

"It's about food and drink," she said, "Soon, we won't have any."

"Come on, dear," she said, lifting her, "You need to rest."

"What's all this?" Fughar asked.

"I had a vision," Vega replied, "It will affect the whole village. But, the Council of Elders never believes me. I need your help convincing them to prepare, or we're all doomed."

His eyes widened, "What did you see?"

"The village is going to suffer a drought," she said, "People had no food, no water. They all had to leave, or die. If the council doesn't prepare for this, that's what will happen."

Fughar stared at her in amazement, brown eyes wide against his bony face. After a long pause, he smiled, "You're not just a psychic; you're an oracle."

"What?" she said.

"I had hoped to find one in my lifetime. That's why I studied them so much, and understood what your episodes were. You only discover whether someone's an oracle or merely psychic when they're ten."

"How?" she asked, confused, "What's an oracle?"

"A psychic has visions of the futures of individuals. They can read people's futures by touching them, and sometimes they receive visions of people they care about without touching them, if they're going to be in danger. But an oracle has visions of individuals *and* groups. They can see what will happen to villages, kingdoms, countries, even the world. They can see the players necessary to prevent widespread tragedy, and they can see individual destinies. They're far more powerful and intuitive than a mere psychic. You've just had your first oracle vision."

Vega sat there, processing what Fughar was telling her. She wasn't sure how to react. After a pause, she said, "So, will you help me talk to the village council?"

"I will speak with them on your behalf," he replied, "But I don't expect much from them at this point. It's hard for people with closed minds to open them enough to believe in things beyond their own senses. We must also warn the people individually. Everyone can make preparations on their own if they believe us. We'll convince as many as we can."

For the next few days, Vega and Fughar spoke with as many villagers as possible, warning them of the impending drought, and trying to convince them to make preparations for it. Fughar also spoke with the Council of Elders. But, as he predicted, they didn't listen.

Several of the people listened, including Miss Geneva and Cassie's family. About half of the village started making preparations in secret, not wanting to attract the attention of the council. They built large containers, hiding them behind huts and barns, which they began stockpiling with water. They started conserving their water usage, keeping it to a minimum.

The other half of the village, including the council, refused to listen, ignoring their warnings. They continued about their lives as normal, not bothering to save up any water, or to cut back on their usage. They were used to frequent rain, and plenty of water from the river, so they saw no impending danger of their supply running out.

It started slow, with no rain for a month. The villagers were still able to get water from the river, so they continued to not worry about it. Vega and her parents were busily conserving water, along with the villagers who believed her. Life was good for the moment, as she continued living in this little town—going to school, playing with kids her own age, and helping her parents run their new farm.

In spite of what she knew was coming, she was happy. And even though the Council of Elders refused to listen, at least a good number of the villagers had. She took comfort in the knowledge that those who'd listened to her would survive this tragedy. Perhaps that's what being an oracle really meant: you could help *change* the future. It wasn't just about being able to see it, but about being able to change it. For the first time, she began to see her visions as a gift rather than a curse. She could use them to help people. She had already used them to prevent two terrible things from happening: one to Cassie and one to Miss Geneva. If being an oracle meant seeing widespread events, imagine the number of people she could help.

When the river began to run low, panic spread across the village. Those who hadn't listened began conserving water, and trying to gather stores from the depleting river. But, they were too late. Eventually, the river ran dry, and the drought set in.

Those who had prepared continued conserving their stores of water, waiting it out. For those who hadn't, their meager stores didn't last long, and they were unable to grow food or bathe, as they had to use what little water they had for drinking.

They began to beg the prepared villagers to help them out, and let them have some of their water. The village council even demanded that they share their stores. But, they refused. They spoke out about how they had refused to listen to the warnings, and now that they were proven wrong, they wanted help. Now, they wanted to share in the resources of those who'd actually prepared. They knew they didn't have enough for everyone, and they didn't want to be forced to leave their home because half of its people had refused to listen to the warnings. No one was sure how long the drought would last.

The Council of Elders shipped off their prisoners to Katangalo's main city for the royals to deal with, so they wouldn't have to provide them food and water. They also had to send representatives to neighboring lands to buy food and water, bringing them back for the suffering people of their village. They began doing everything they could to survive the drought.

When her vision was proven right, people began coming to Vega to have her read their futures. It didn't always work, but she was sometimes able to see people's futures when she touched them. Fughar said it was for three reasons. One: she had only just become an oracle, and she needed a lot of practice before she would become experienced enough to fully understand her visions. Two: visions are unpredictable. You can only see what you are meant to see. And three: not everyone has a significant future. If nothing out of the ordinary will happen to them, there's nothing to see.

For some reason, whenever she touched Cassie, she had a vision. The first time was her vision of her being attacked. The second was her vision of the drought. She began to see a pattern when Cassie asked her to read her future.

"I just want to know what my life will be like," she said, looking at her earnestly, gray eyes pleading.

"That's not how it works," Vega replied, "I never know what I'll see, if anything."

"Come on," she said, "Just try it . . . pleaasee?"

She sighed, "Very well." She took her hand, and immediately blacked out. She was standing in the town square. But everything looked different. The huts were bigger, and seemed to be better-made. None of the people looked familiar. Then, she saw a young man. He looked just like Cassie: brown, curly hair and gray eyes. He looked miserable. As she watched, he led his brown stallion from the village, and, as soon as he'd ridden over the hill into Millhaymae, he smiled.

She came to rather quickly this time. After so many readings, her body had begun to handle her visions better. She no longer got severe headaches, and she wasn't blacked out for nearly as long. She still got minor headaches, though. She tried to limit the number of readings she did to two a day.

"Well, what did you see?" Cassie asked eagerly.

"I'm not sure," Vega replied.

She frowned, disappointed.

"I saw a young man. He looked just like you. He rode out of the village on his horse, and he smiled."

"Who was it?" she asked, "My father? My brother?"

"No," she replied, "I don't know who he was. I've never seen him before." She paused, "The village looked different, too. I didn't recognize anyone. The huts were bigger, and better-made."

Cassie furrowed her brow in confusion, "How far in the future can you see?"

"I don't know," she said, "I'm still learning about my visions as I go."

"Maybe he's my son," she said.

"Maybe," Vega answered, "I honestly have no idea."

Every time she read her future after that, she saw the same man. In one, he was working on a farm. It appeared to be in the same place as Cassie's hut, but it looked different. In another, he was in the library, studying. The library looked different, too. It had a far larger selection of books. Vega wished she could read them. He was reading a book on the elemental birds: phoenixes, dwervas, auristras, and dirthens. He was like them, with a love of learning.

Each time she had a vision of him, she waited to hear a name, but she never did. It was frustrating for her, seeing him over and over, and never learning who he was. All she knew was that he was important for some reason, and that he was associated with Cassie.

She began sketching him, countless drawings of this unnamed man filling her room. She showed them to Cassie, so she could see what he looked like. She had never seen him before, so they knew he wasn't a current member of her family.

Vega sketched him for months, before the drought finally ended. She was sitting in her room, spiraling her pencil around to form his curly hair, when she heard *plinks* of water against her window. She gasped in disbelief, rising from her spot on the floor and looking outside. She smiled broadly as she saw that it was raining. More than that, it was pouring. The dry, barren, dirt roads of the village were being flooded with water.

It rained all night. The next morning, when the sun came out, Vega ventured outside. Trudging through the thick layer of mud from the flooding the night before, she saw several of the villagers who'd been starving and dehydrating outside cheering. They'd filled reservoirs in the night with water, to ensure they would still have some in the days to come.

As she looked around, smiling, Elder Danvers approached her. "Vega," he said, "The Council of Elders would like to speak with you."

She reluctantly followed him to Town Hall, and they entered the large hut where the council assembled. Elder Khantis opened his arms in greeting, "Vega! Wonderful to see you!"

She looked at him in disbelief. She was sure her disgust for him was visible on her face, but she didn't care. He was the reason her visions were never believed. Now, he suddenly wanted to be nice to her?

"I know I haven't been what you needed in the past," he said, "But, I'd like to change that in the future." He paused, "I called you here to thank you. You saved the village. If not for half the people preparing for this drought, we wouldn't have had the funds to provide for everyone. Many would have died, or been forced to relocate. I'm grateful that some of our people listened to you, even when we didn't."

Vega faltered, unsure what to say. She hadn't expected an apology from him. His gratitude took her by surprise.

"Fughar says you're an oracle," Elder Khantis continued, "I'd like to ask you to become our official village oracle."

She still didn't say anything. She wasn't sure how to process his request. Becoming the village oracle? Even she knew this was bigger than she could probably understand.

"What do you say?" he asked.

"I need to think about it," she said, "And discuss it with my parents."

"Of course," he said quickly, "Why don't you just give me your answer by the end of the week? You'll be turning eleven soon, if I'm not mistaken. You could start a new year with a new title. Think about it."

Vega nodded, hurrying out of Town Hall. She went straight to Fughar's hut, not knowing who else to go to.

"Vega?" the frail old medicine man said when she entered, "What is it?"

"Elder Khantis wants me to become the village oracle," she said, "I'm not sure if I should."

Fughar's eyes widened, "Absolutely not!"

She looked up at him in surprise at his outburst.

He calmed himself, kneeling before her to reach her level, "Vega, you must not become the village oracle. Elder Khantis would use you to gain power. Having an oracle is a huge advantage in times of conflict. Many would seek to use you for their own ends, including him. You must not allow yourself to be dedicated to any kingdom. You must be dedicated to yourself. You must make your own decisions, and use your gift how you see fit to use it. It can be a burden, with so many people vying for your power, but you must be strong. Trust me."

She nodded, "But, what do I tell Elder Khantis?"

"Nothing," he said, "You must not speak of this to anyone."

"But, he wants an answer by the end of the week," Vega said anxiously.

Fughar sighed, "Then, you have a week to get your affairs in order. Elder Khantis will be very upset if you refuse. Who knows what he would do. You must leave Katangalo."

"What?" she exclaimed, "But, this is my home, now."

"I know," he said, "But your powers can't fall into the wrong hands. Being an oracle is a burden and a responsibility. It's a curse as much as a gift. I know you want to be a normal kid, but you're not. You never will be. You must trust me on this. You must find a safe place to call home. I'm afraid I cannot tell you where you should go. I only know you can no longer stay." He sighed again, looking away, "Your parents may not understand. But, you must leave here no matter what . . . whether they go with you, or . . . "

"Or what?"

"You go alone," he said finally.

"I'm ten years old!" she yelled.

"I'm aware," he replied, "But, oracles do not have the luxury of being anything but what they are." After another pause, he said, "If your parents say no, I'll go with you."

Vega looked at him, "You'll . . . what?"

"I'll go with you," he said, "So you're not alone. But, you must leave this village before the week is up."

Garellis

4

"Arenelle! No!" shouted a man with silver hair, blue eyes, pointed ears, and angular features.

A young girl who resembled him was standing there, holding up a little flower, and a man in a black cloak was casting a spell at her. She fell when it hit her, and Vega could see she was dead.

The man ran toward them, tears streaming down, a desperate rage in his eyes.

"Irvenix!" a woman behind him shouted, holding a preteen boy close to her chest. They were both crying as well.

Before he could reach the wizard, he waved his wand, disappearing from sight.

"No!" Irvenix yelled again. He collapsed to the ground beside the little girl, wrapping her in his arms. He looked up at the woman, weakly saying, "Irena."

She came closer to him, clinging to the boy the whole way.

"I will avenge her death," Irvenix said, "For you, my wife, and you, my son."

"No," Irena said, "You're not a wizard. We'll only lose you, too."

He got up wordlessly, a look in his eyes that frightened Vega. He headed into the forest, not looking back.

Irena broke down in tears, placing a shaky hand on the little girl's body. She looked up at the boy, "I'm so sorry, Aurano."

Vega looked around her darkened bedroom, a strange feeling coming over her. It combined with the sadness of what she'd seen, and she suddenly had clarity. She knew what she had to do. Up 'til then, she hadn't been sure. Deep down, she knew Fughar was right, but she didn't want to leave. She let loose a few tears in the darkness, mentally saying *goodbye* to the happy life she'd grown to love.

When morning came, Vega got up, packing a bag and making her way to Fughar's hut. When she walked inside, he gave her a knowing look, not saying anything. He grabbed his bag and led her to the stall beside his hut, which housed his horse. They loaded up their bags, and he climbed into the saddle, helping her up behind him.

"Where to?" he asked.

"The land of the elves," she replied.

He shook the reins, and they set out north, toward Gliken.

Being an oracle meant she could never have a normal life. An eleven-year-old leaving her parents was a thing unheard of, and yet she had no choice. They would never understand. Her power made her more than just a girl. She could never fully experience a human life.

"Did you have a vision?" Fughar asked from in front of her on the horse.

"Yes," Vega replied, "An elven girl is going to be killed by a dark wizard. Her father is going to try to avenge her death, but he's not a wizard."

He gasped, "You had a vision of elves without ever seeing one before?"

"Well, I saw pictures of them in books . . ."

"That's incredible," he said, "You are a very powerful oracle indeed."

Vega wasn't sure how to respond, so she sat quietly, looking off into the forest on either side of the grassy clearing they were traversing.

When it got dark, they stopped to make camp, Fughar cooking a meager meal for the two of them. "We should reach Gliken by lunchtime tomorrow," he said, "Hopefully, the king will hear your vision."

She nodded, lost in her own thoughts, *What am I supposed to say? If I'm going to be an oracle, I need to be more eloquent. I wish I could still attend school . . .*

The next day, as Fughar had said, they reached Gliken by lunchtime. She knew thanks to all she'd learned of the elves in Miss Geneva's after-school sessions. The trees were more ancient and magical, and the air was wet with mist. The tiny droplets stuck to her hair, beading it with dew. They didn't get far before a line of elves on horseback appeared before them. Vega knew they were the guardians of the kingdom of Garellis.

"Halt!" the head guard said, coming forward. He had pale skin, silver hair, and a stern expression. "What brings you here?" he demanded.

"We come seeking guidance," Fughar said, "And, we come bearing a message for your king."

They looked at each other, unsure. Finally, he said, "Come with me."

He led them through the misty forest and to the realm of the elves. It was even more beautiful and magical than the pictures. The tree structures that formed their homes and buildings were truly incredible in real life. All around her, the forest was full of life. She saw pixies darting about, dwervas and auristras soaring through the air, and she even caught a glimpse of a mermaid.

They entered the magnificent tree palace of the elf-king, and were led through the viny corridors to the throne room. It was overwhelmingly large and beautiful. They dismounted their horse, standing before the king. He had pale skin and silver hair like the guard, and wore a shimmering robe that changed from purple to white to blue before her very eyes.

"What's this?" he asked, looking at them steadily.

"Messengers," the guard said, bowing.

"Messengers?" he repeated, "What message do a frail old man and a young girl bring before King Jurien of Garellis?"

"She is an oracle, sire," Fughar said, "She has had a vision concerning your people she wishes to share, in hopes of preventing a tragedy."

King Jurien looked at her steadily, "Oracle, you say?"

He nodded.

"Very well," he said, sitting back on his throne, "What is this *vision*?"

Vega cleared her throat nervously, "A dark elven wizard is going to kill a young girl." After a pause, she added, "Her name is Arenelle."

He scoffed, "Unlikely. There are no dark elven wizards in Gliken. Dark wizards reside in Kogatsa. Furthermore, none could get through our warriors. We have several wizards in our company for protection from things such as this. They would never be near any civilians." He paused, "You are young. Perhaps your visions aren't fully developed yet."

"Visions aren't things that develop with age," Fughar inserted, "She hasn't been wrong in her predictions before. You would be wise to listen to her."

"You dare to address a king in that manner?" he said, angry, "You think a human counselor is warranted here? That you can waltz right into the domain of elves, and tell *us* what to do?"

"But, the girl!" Vega pleaded.

"Silence!" King Jurien said, rising, "Enough of this foolishness. Gerard, get them out of my sight."

The guard bowed his head in acknowledgment, coming forward. He led them from the room, as they reluctantly followed.

"Sir," Vega said once they were outside, "That girl is in danger."

"I'm sorry," he said, "I cannot defy the orders of my king to help you." He paused, "But, he didn't say anything about finding you a place to stay . . ."

"That would be wonderful," Fughar said, "We'd very much appreciate it."

Vega hung her head as they followed Gerard through the elven kingdom. He led them across the grassy clearing in the center of the city, and up a staircase made from interwoven branches. He knocked on the door, waiting.

Finally, a beautiful, silver-haired elven woman answered, "Yes?" She looked over the two of them uncertainly. When her eyes landed on the guard, she said, "Oh, Gerard! Come in!"

The two of them followed the guard inside as the woman's eyes scrutinized them. It was a library, with hundreds of books stocking the natural shelves formed by the trees. There were little nooks for reading, with chairs formed from plant life. Vega wondered if everything the elves owned was made from the forest itself.

"Jezebelle," Gerard said, "These two need a place to stay. I was wondering if maybe . . ."

She sighed, rolling her eyes, "How long?"

He smiled, "Thank you." Then, he turned to Vega and Fughar, "How long do the two of you plan to stay?"

"Uh . . . " Fughar began, looking at Vega, "I'm not sure. We don't exactly have a place to call home."

"I'm sorry," Jezebelle said, "But, humans cannot live in the land of the elves."

"How about a couple of weeks, then?"

She sighed again, "Very well. You may stay here for a fortnight."

"Thank you," he said, bowing his head slightly.

"Well, I've got to get back to work," Gerard said, "But, thank you again, Jezebelle." He gave her a quick hug and kiss, heading out of the library.

She looked the two of them over again before finally saying, "What are your names?"

"I am Fughar, and this is Vega."

"Is she your granddaughter?" she asked.

His eyes widened, "Oh, no. We're not related. We are only traveling together."

"A young girl and an old man?" she questioned skeptically.

"Yes. She is an—"

"I'm an oracle," Vega interrupted, "And he is a medicine man. He's accompanying me on my travels, so I'm not alone."

"I see," she said, "So, he is your keeper?"

Vega looked at her in confusion.

Jezebelle smiled, "You're not a very experienced oracle yet, are you?"

"I'm only eleven," she replied.

She chuckled, "Yes. I always forget how quickly humans age." She paused, "Most oracles have a keeper. They are tasked with caring for them, protecting them, and facilitating their communications with those who come seeking their foresight."

"Then, yes," Fughar said, "I am her keeper."

"What brings you to the land of the elves?" she asked curiously.

"I came to warn you," Vega said, "I had a vision of one of your people. But, your king will not listen to me."

Jezebelle bristled, looking wary, "What was your vision?"

"A young girl is going to be killed by a dark wizard," Fughar said.

"Do you know who it is?" she asked worriedly.

Vega looked up, "Her name is Arenelle."

She gasped, but remained silent. After a long pause, she said, "Let me show you to your rooms."

They followed her through the elven library, through a door, and down a winding staircase to a short corridor.

"This is the bathroom," she said, tapping the first door, "This is my room. These two will be your rooms while you're here."

"Thank you," Fughar said again, nodding.

"I'll let you get settled," she said, giving them a nod and heading back up the stairs.

They went into the rooms, and the beds were made from plant life like the chairs. Vega stared at it skeptically, unsure about sleeping on plants. This whole place was strange, and she was almost glad humans weren't welcome. She didn't think she could stay there forever. But, in the meantime, she wondered what else Jezebelle could teach her about oracles. She seemed knowledgeable on the subject. With an entire elven library above her, at least she could do some studying.

The next few days Vega spent reading every book she could in the incredible elven library. Fughar spent his time talking to some of the elves, and trying to find Irvenix and Irena, the parents of the little girl in Vega's vision. Jezebelle was the elven librarian, and she spent her time cleaning and organizing the library, and helping any elves who came looking for a book. At first, she seemed annoyed at having humans staying with her, and she made her disdain for their inferior education obvious. But, as the days went by, she took a liking to Vega, as she watched her devour every book on her shelves.

"I'm impressed by your eagerness to learn," Jezebelle said, "I've never seen anyone—elf or otherwise—read all of the books I have here."

"I love to read," Vega replied, "Growing up, I never got to attend school, as my parents were worried about my 'episodes,' which I later discovered were visions. I finally got to attend a year of school in Kataran, and the teacher helped me catch up on the material I'd missed. But, now I won't be able to attend school again. I can't ever have a normal life. So, I'm determined to learn as much as I can when I have the opportunity to."

She looked at her sympathetically. After a pause, she said, "I want to show you something."

She looked up at the elven librarian curiously.

"Come with me," she said, offering her hand.

Vega took it, following Jezebelle out of the library. They walked into the elven forest, and she led her through the ancient, mystical trees, and through a wall of vines, into a clearing. When they stepped into it, she saw the largest tree she'd ever seen in her life. It spanned almost the entirety of the massive clearing, its roots visible in places as they spread into the forest around them. It towered high into the sky, its branches fanning over them like a massive umbrella. Something felt strange about the tree. It almost seemed to glow, and Vega swore she could see beams of light radiating along its roots.

"What is it?" she asked in awe.

"This is the Tree of Knowledge," Jezebelle replied, "It is the source of all life and knowledge since the beginning of time. The wisdom and life forces of every generation eventually wind up within this tree. It is the beating heart of the forest. We are all connected to it, even while we are alive."

She gawked at it in awe, venturing a little closer. She had read a few things about the Tree of Knowledge before, but she had never imagined it quite like this.

"Place your hand upon the trunk," she said, giving her a nod.

Vega inched forward uncertainly. As she did, she tripped over a root, face-planting in the grass. When she looked up, there was a young elven girl standing over her, looking at her curiously. She had dark skin, black hair, and brown eyes.

"Are you a human?" she asked in wonder.

She smiled at the girl, "Yes, sort of."

"Sort of?" she asked, confused.

"I'm an oracle," she replied, "My name's Vega."

The girl's eyes widened, "An oracle? Really? Wow!"

"Vega, are you alright?" Jezebelle asked, coming up beside them.

She nodded.

"Oh, let me help you up," the girl said, pulling her to her feet, "I'm Kamine, by the way."

"Nice to meet you," she said.

"Kamine," Jezebelle reprimanded, "Don't let your curiosity impede your manners."

"Sorry," she said, staring at her feet guiltily.

"It's alright," Vega said, "I know I was amazed the first time I saw an elf in person."

Kamine smiled, "We are pretty different."

Jezebelle shook her head, "Kamine is very studious, not unlike yourself. She spends a lot of time at the library. She spends the rest here, at the Tree of Knowledge."

"You can learn a lot here," she said excitedly, "More than in books, even."

"Really?" Vega asked, "This tree *is* amazing."

Kamine nodded.

"I've got to get back to the library," Jezebelle said, "Kamine, why don't you take Vega with you? It would be good for both of you to get out more."

As she walked away, Kamine said, "Come on, I'll introduce you to my sisters."

"Um, sure," Vega said uncertainly.

"Don't worry, they're awesome," she said, taking her hand.

She followed the young, dark elf girl through the forest, and out into a grove with a few houses built into the trees. They went up the winding staircase, and into one of the houses. Inside, all of the shelves, artwork, and even appliances were formed from the trees themselves. The furniture was all made from plant life. The land of the elves was both magical and unusual.

"Gizella! Xharia!" Kamine shouted, searching the hall, "Where are you?"

The house remained quiet, and Vega looked around at the family portraits of Kamine and her older sisters with their parents. It made her think of the family from her vision, and she grew sad, wishing the king would listen to her.

"I guess they're not home," Kamine said finally, "Xharia's probably off training. She wants to be an elven warrior one day. Gizella and my mother must be out."

"What about your father?" Vega asked.

"Oh, he's on a quest right now. He won't be home for a while. Come on!" With that, she grabbed Vega's hand and started sprinting out of the house. They ran through the forest again, and to the river. They sat upon the edge, looking into the crystal clear water.

"What are we doing now?"

"Shh!" Kamine whispered, "Just wait."

They sat staring into the water for what seemed like a long time. Finally, they saw shimmering purple scales beneath the surface.

"Whoa!" Vega whispered, "What was that?"

Kamine just smiled.

As they watched, a mermaid surfaced on the opposite bank, her purple hair flowing over her.

"Wow," Vega said in amazement, staring at her.

"Melina!" Kamine called, waving.

The mermaid turned her head in surprise, looking fearful for a moment. When she saw Kamine, she smiled, waving back.

"They can't talk," she said, "But they're very friendly. At least, most of them."

"How do you know her name, then?"

"Oh, I sort of named them," she said shyly, letting out a nervous giggle, "They responded well to the names. I only know a few of them. They're very shy, and slow to trust. Most of them don't like coming to the surface at all. I bring them food to lure them up, and I try to talk to them through signs and gestures. Mostly, they just listen to me talk. They're very good listeners. I'm not sure they always understand, but it's better than talking to myself."

"That's amazing," Vega said, waving to Melina.

The mermaid looked at her uncertainly, but finally waved to her as well.

"You wanna see something else?" she asked excitedly.

"Sure," Vega replied, smiling.

Kamine was so full of joy and wonder that it made her finally feel like a kid again. Her worries left her as they skipped through the forest, and to a small grove full of pixies. In the shady grove, the pixies shone brightly, lighting the whole area in a beautiful array of colors.

"It's magical!" she exclaimed, holding her arms out to either side and twirling.

Kamine beamed, joining her.

The two girls collapsed on the grass, looking up at the colorful pixies.

"They say pixies can help you with their magic," she said.

"Really?" Vega asked, "How?"

"When they like you, and you really need it, they can help. Magic is one of those things you never can fully understand. It works in mysterious ways. Especially when it comes to magical creatures. They can be very unpredictable."

Vega closed her eyes, willing the pixies to help save Arenelle with their magic. *I don't know if this will work,* she thought, *But, I have to try . . .*

Boreas

5

"Vega, wake up," Fughar whispered, shaking her.

"Wh-what is it?" she asked groggily, rubbing her eyes.

"It's Arenelle," he answered.

Vega jumped up, panicking, "What happened?"

Fughar shook his head sadly.

In her heart, she knew what that meant. Her chest tightened, and a tear formed in her eye, rolling down her cheek.

"I'm sorry," he said, "I tried to find them. I really did."

Vega began sobbing, wiping tears from her eyes and snot from her nose. Fughar hugged her, and she leaned into the old man, taking solace in her only familiar.

"There is talk among the elves of overthrowing King Jurien. Enough of them knew of your prophecy, and how he didn't listen to it. And, it seems, they have quite an extensive list of other reasons as well."

"Good," she replied, wiping her face angrily, "He should be overthrown. Because of him, a little girl had to die."

"Yes, but I fear things are about to get dangerous for us here. We should leave."

"No," Vega said, "We are still needed here." After a pause, she added, "What of Irvenix?"

Fughar sighed, "He has taken a group of elven wizards and warriors to track the dark wizard down and exact his revenge." After another pause, he said, "Her brother, Aurano has not taken it well, either. Though he is too young to accompany his father, he has become an elven warrior-in-training. Poor Irena doesn't know how to handle the situation. She's mourning her daughter, praying for her husband, and trying to care for her son."

"Who will take up the throne if they overthrow Jurien?"

"There are a few possibilities," a voice from the doorway said suddenly.

The two of them jumped, looking over to see that it was Jezebelle.

"But, it will be a struggle for power," she continued, "Fughar's right— it's too dangerous for you to stay."

"How long have you been standing there?" he asked.

She smiled, though they could barely see it in the darkened room, "Long enough."

"We can't leave," Vega said stubbornly, "We're needed here."

Jezebelle looked at her then, "No, young oracle. You must go."

As she opened her mouth to object, she felt weak and faint. She sat back on the bed as she was struck with a vision. It unfolded differently from her previous visions. She was standing in the blackness, unable to see what was happening.

"No!" a woman screamed, "Irvenix!" Broken sobs cut through the darkness.

Through tears, a pubescent boy spoke with determination, "Don't worry, mother. One day, I shall avenge him. The dark wizard, Nazirdok will pay for this!"

"No, Aurano!" she replied, "I won't lose you, too."

"You won't lose me, mother," he said softly, "But, he must pay for what he's done."

Their voices muffled and faded away as light cut through the darkness. She was standing in the throne room of the palace. She turned toward the doorway as she heard someone enter. When she looked, she could see a pale elf with silver hair and armor entering. It took her a moment to realize that it was Aurano. He was all grown up.

"You wished to see me, sire?" he said, kneeling.

"Yes," said a voice from behind her. She turned back toward the throne. But, it was not King Jurien who sat upon it. A dark-skinned elf with black hair and brown eyes sat there instead. He looked vaguely familiar, but Vega couldn't say why. "You performed well in the tournament today," he said, "As the elven warrior of The Great Prophecy, I expect you to bring honor to the elves."

"Yes, sire," Aurano replied.

"I know you will," he said, "My daughter, Xharia tells me you are the most dedicated warrior-in-training she has ever seen." He paused, "If you do well on this quest, you may very well earn the title of elven warrior."

He looked up, "That is all I've worked my whole life for."

"Good," he said, nodding, "Dismissed. Rest up, and meet the princess and her human warrior by the horses at dawn."

Once he'd said the name of his daughter, Vega realized who he was. It was Kamine's father! Suddenly, she understood the significance of what she'd seen. He would become the new king when Jurien was overthrown!

As her vision faded away, she could see Fughar and Jezebelle patiently waiting for her to tell them what she'd seen. She sat silently for a moment, catching her breath, and replaying what she'd seen in her mind.

"What did you see?" Fughar asked finally.

"I know who the new king is going to be," she replied.

The next few days, Vega spent her time with Kamine, hoping to finally meet the rest of her family, and wondering when her father would return from his quest.

"Melina, you've met," Kamine said, gesturing to the purple mermaid, "This is Sasha, Sabrina, and Reina," she gestured to the blue mermaid, then the pink one, and finally, the yellow one.

The two of them were on the bank of the river, where the mermaids were relaxing on the shore. They were all beautiful, magical beings, and Vega would normally have been entranced to meet them. But, her mind was preoccupied with thoughts of her latest vision.

"Vega," Kamine said, snapping her out of her thoughts, "Are you alright?"

"Y-yes, I'm fine. What were you saying?"

"I was introducing you to the other mermaids, and you didn't say anything," she looked at her disapprovingly.

"Oh, I'm sorry," she replied quickly, "It's a pleasure to meet all of you." After an awkward pause, she said, "So . . . what's it like, living underwater?"

Kamine shook her head. The mermaids, on the other hand, smiled and started splashing. The two girls laughed and splashed with them, getting completely soaked. Vega forgot her troubles, feeling like a kid again as she splashed and laughed and played with her new friend and a group of mermaids. Suddenly, the mermaids dove back into the river, seeming frightened. The two girls looked at each other in confusion. Then, they heard the horns.

The young elf looked up, "Father? Father! He's back!"

Vega looked up with interest as she saw the group of elves returning from their quest. She recognized Kamine's father immediately, after her vision. She also noticed the group of warriors had a human in their midst. He was tall, with tan skin, brown eyes and hair, and a crown upon his head.

"Who's he?" she asked curiously.

"I don't know," the dark elven girl answered, "I've never seen a human here before."

Vega followed her as she ran up to the warriors, straight for her father. When he saw her, he flashed a huge smile, running forward to meet her, and wrapping her in his arms.

"Kamine! How have you been, my child?"

"I've been good! I've been studying mermaids and pixies! How was your quest?"

"It was successful," he replied, turning serious. After a pause, he said, "Who's your friend?"

"This is Vega. She's an oracle."

"An oracle, you say?" he asked curiously, looking her over, "How came you to the land of the elves?"

"I came to warn your king of a vision I had, where a young elven girl was killed. But, he refused to listen. Now, it has come true. And, the people have begun talk of overthrowing King Jurien."

"So, it's finally happening," he said, looking to the warriors around him. He turned back to her, "Who was the girl?"

"Arenelle, daughter of Irena and Irvenix," she replied.

His eyes widened, "Aurano is friends with my daughter, Xharia." After a horrified pause, he added, "Arenelle was close to Kamine's age." He looked at his daughter, and Vega could see the worry in his face.

"I'm sorry, Boreas," the human man said.

"This could have been avoided," Boreas said, "But, Jurien refuses to do his duty. He will not listen to his subjects, or even his council. If what this young oracle says is true, then it is truly time he was relieved of power."

"And, who will be king in his place?" one of the elven warriors asked pointedly, "You?"

"Of course not," Boreas said, "But, someone who would care for the interests of our people, better than Jurien."

"Why *not* you?" another warrior asked, "I'd vote for you. I'd follow you anywhere."

"I'm flattered, Thaddeus," he said, "But, I'm no ruler. I'm just like any of you."

"That's exactly why it should be you," he replied, "You care for us, because you're one of us."

Boreas waved his hand, dismissing his statement, "Whomever the people decide on to rule is yet to be determined. All we now know is that Jurien must be overthrown."

As the other warriors started arguing amongst themselves, he took his daughter's hand, "Let's go home. I cannot wait a moment longer to see your mother and sisters."

Kamine beamed, skipping beside him, "Come on, Vega! I want you to meet everyone!"

She followed, both anxious to meet everyone, and unsure if it was her place. They left the rest of the warriors behind as the three of them headed for their house. As soon as they opened the door, a dark-skinned elven woman launched herself into Boreas' arms.

"Boreas!" she said, holding him tight.

"Annalisa," he said contentedly, wrapping his arms around her.

She looked down at her daughter then, "Kamine! Where have you been?"

"I was just play—"

"Get in the house, now," she ordered, pointing inside.

As the two girls entered, Boreas said, "Aw, Annalisa, let her be a kid."

"Don't start," she replied. She sighed, "I'm just so happy you're back. I always worry when you're gone."

"I know," he said, "I have so much to tell you."

"Father!" came the yell of two girls, as they shoved each other out of the way to come down the stairs into the kitchen where they were all standing. One of them was a preteen with black hair and intense hazel eyes. Vega

44

guessed she was Xharia, as she appeared close in age to Aurano. The other girl looked like a teenager. By default, she guessed she was Gizella. She had black hair and brown eyes like the rest of her family, besides their mother, who had hazel eyes as well.

Boreas held his arms wide open as the two girls plowed into him. He hugged them tight, saying, "My beautiful daughters! How have you been?"

"I've been good, father," Gizella said, "Mother and I have been attending *all* the social events this season. We found several new gowns for me to wear!"

"I've been training," Xharia said, rolling her eyes at her sister, "Perhaps I can compete in the tournament next week?"

He sighed, "We'll see."

"Xharia," Annalisa snapped, "Can you let him get settled before you start asking for things?"

"Sorry, mother," she replied.

It was then that they noticed Vega, standing beside Kamine.

"Who's this?" their mother asked.

As Kamine opened her mouth to introduce her, Boreas said, "She's an oracle. She prophesied what happened to Arenelle."

Annalisa's eyes widened, "How do you know about that? You've been gone."

"She told me," he said.

They all looked at her, then.

"We have to overthrow Jurien," Boreas said, breaking the silence.

"What?" Annalisa asked, shocked, "No. Absolutely not. You just got back. You are not starting a war campaign now."

"Annalisa, I—"

"No," she inserted, "Now, it is time for dinner. We are going to sit as a family, and eat the meal I've prepared." She looked at Vega, "You are welcome to join us, so long as you do not discuss anything related to politics or prophecies."

With that, she walked over to the stove and began serving up plates, "Set the table, Gizella."

The rest of them sat silently at the table as the food was served. Delicately prepared elven fruits and vegetables adorned the plates, with several rolls placed in the center of the table. They ate in awkward silence, no one wanting to be the first to talk.

When they'd finished, Annalisa and Gizella began clean-up, and Boreas gestured for Vega to follow him outside. Kamine and Xharia followed as well, and they made their way down the winding staircase, and out of earshot of the house.

"I was wondering if you could read the future," he said, "I just want to know whether we succeed in overthrowing Jurien."

Vega looked at him. She could tell he was a good man. A man who put his family and the elven people above himself and above power. She knew he would make a good king, for the simple fact that he didn't want to be king. But, she didn't think she should tell him what she'd seen. After a long pause, she said, "Yes. King Jurien will be overthrown."

He smiled, shaking her hand, "Thank you."

The moment he touched her, she felt another vision coming on. Their whole family had an air of destiny about them, and she wasn't sure whether that meant she should hang around them or avoid them. There was no sound this time in her vision. She saw herself, riding with Fughar upon his horse. As she watched, she saw Boreas and the human man riding up on either side of them. They were headed through the elven forest toward the land of the dwarves. She wasn't sure why, but it felt right, like that was what they were supposed to be doing.

When she came out of her trance, the dark elven man and his two daughters were staring at her worriedly. "Are you alright?" Kamine asked.

She nodded. As many visions as she'd been having lately, she was starting to get more used to them. They didn't affect her as much as they had before, and she was able to recover more quickly. She looked at Boreas, "I saw us, riding toward Korga. My keeper, Fughar, was with us. And, that human man who accompanied you earlier."

He looked surprised, and then he gazed off into the forest, obviously unsure how to process what she'd just told him. Finally, he asked, "Why?"

"I'm not sure," she replied, "But, it felt right. Like, that's what we're *supposed* to do."

"When do we leave?"

"I don't know that, either," she said, "But, I would guess as soon as possible."

"What?" Kamine shouted, "But, you just got back!"

"He's a warrior, Kamine," Xharia said, "Sometimes, there are things he has to do that he doesn't want to do. One day, when you're older, you will understand."

"How would you know, Xharia?" she demanded, upset.

"Girls, please," he said, "Everything will be alright. Times are getting dangerous for all of us right now. If I am to keep you safe, I must make some tough calls. Our king let a little girl die. That could have been one of you. He cannot remain king if those are the kinds of decisions he makes. A king should put his people first. He should prevent unnecessary deaths, not ignore them. He ignored this young oracle's advice. I shall not follow his example."

"I shall let Fughar know," Vega said, nodding.

"We leave in three days' time," Boreas replied, "I want to have at least that long with my family."

The Tree of Knowledge

6

"I want to show you something," Jezebelle said, waving Vega over. She followed the silver-haired elf to a large object on three legs, with a long cylinder pointed upwards at the skylight in the roof of the library.

"What is it?" Vega asked.

"This?" Jezebelle replied, pointing at the object, "This is a telescope. It allows you to see the stars. Many elven scientists have observed them for centuries, learning countless things about our world. But that's not what I wanted to show you. I wanted to show you what I've been observing through it, ever since you had that vision about Boreas becoming king."

Vega stepped forward as she showed her where to place her eye to see through the telescope. She could see a bunch of dust clouds near a bright, shining star. When she stepped back, she said, "Dust in space?"

Jezebelle shook her head, "They're gas clouds. That star you see is new. It formed the night you had your vision. And, it appears there will be more to follow."

She gasped, "What are you saying? They're somehow related to my visions? There will be more of them soon?"

"I'm not sure," she replied, "I do not know whether they are related. I only know that the first one formed that night."

Her eyes widened as she tried to process what she was being told.

"Listen," Jezebelle said, "I don't tell everyone this, but I'm an elven witch. I know you're leaving soon, and I want to give you something to take on your travels." She pulled out a silvery mirror with an intricate design of leaves and vines on the back, "Here." After a pause, she asked, "Do you know what this is?"

She shook her head.

"It's a witch's glass. Take it with you, and I'll be able to call you upon it while you're traveling. I can tell you whenever another star forms, and we shall see if they correlate with your visions."

"Wow. Thank you," Vega said, clutching the mirror to her chest.

Jezebelle gave her a deep nod, "Good luck, Vega. It's been a pleasure."

With only one more day before they would depart, Vega wanted to talk to Kamine. She had been distant since she had asked her father to accompany her on the road, and she wanted to make things right. She went to her house and knocked on the door.

Her mother, Annalisa, answered, looking at her in irritation, "What do you want?"

"Is Kamine home?"

"No, she's not," she replied, "And neither is my husband, no thanks to you. He just got home, and on some whim, you want him to accompany you?"

Vega was silent.

"Don't come around here again," she said, "You've done enough." With that, she slammed the door in her face.

Vega stood there a moment, unable to move. She never wanted to hurt their family. She realized her visions would always have control. Though she knew she could never have a normal life, she wanted nothing more than to help others, not hurt them. Finally, she walked away, to try and find Kamine. She knew she wasn't at the library, so she went to the river to see if she was chatting with the mermaids.

When she wasn't there, she headed to the grove of pixies. They flitted about, frightened by the way she burst into the grove to look for her friend. She wasn't there, either. Her last hope was the Tree of Knowledge. She ran back out of the grove, headed straight there. Suddenly, she ran into her father, Boreas.

"Vega," he said in surprise, "What are you doing here?"

"I-uh, I was looking for Kamine," she replied. It was then she noticed the human man from before was with him.

"I'd like to introduce you to someone," Boreas said, gesturing toward him, "This is Boreas."

Vega looked at them in confusion.

They burst into laughter, "Yes, we're both named Boreas. He is the king of the kingdom of Ivonneveille in the land of Duwazo."

"Pleasure to meet you," King Boreas said, holding out his hand.

She shook it, glad to finally meet the fourth member of their soon-to-be travel party. As she did so, everything faded away, and she was standing in the throne room of a palace. A young woman was there, with long, light blonde hair and blue eyes, garbed in a peasant's dress. A woman with light brown skin and caramel hair sat upon the throne. She wore a lavender ball-gown and a gold tiara. It was then she saw him—the man from the visions she'd had through Cassie.

"Celestia!" the woman exclaimed, rushing from her throne toward her. They embraced as she said, "I'm so sorry. I should've told you. I should've told you about your father."

"It's okay, mother," Celestia said, "I'm sorry, too."

The young man began to back out of the room. *No,* Vega thought, *Who are you? How are you connected to Cassie?*

"And, who's this gentleman?" the queen asked, as if reading her thoughts.

"This is Bridgot," Celestia said, "I have so much to tell you, mother. To make a long story short, after I ran away, I discovered I'm the princess of an ancient prophecy, destined to save the world from darkness, with the help of a human warrior, an elven warrior, and a dwarven warrior. We also had help from a dragon rider. I've seen so many unbelievable things, I don't know if you'd ever believe them, mother. But, Bridgot is my human warrior. He saved my life more than once. I wouldn't be standing here without him."

The throne room faded away, and she was back in Kataran. But, it didn't look like the Kataran she'd lived in. It looked like the Kataran from

Bridgot's time. Now that she knew his name, she wished she could tell it to Cassie.

Just then, she saw Bridgot, running forward with a smile, "Grandma Cassie!"

Vega saw her old friend then, an old woman. She was wrinkled; her brown curls turned gray to match her eyes. She hardly recognized her. An old man walked past in the next room at the same time, and she assumed it was her husband. After a moment, she recognized him as Marcus—one of the boys from their after-school sessions!

"Oh, my dear Bridgot," she said as they embraced, "It's so good to see you."

"I did it, grandma," he said, stepping back from her arms, "I did it."

"I heard," she said, "Good for you. You've always had a head on your shoulders. If anyone could solve an 'unsolvable riddle,' it's you."

"But, I'm not warrior material, grandmother," he replied, "Nobody thinks so. How can I protect a princess as she fulfills an ancient prophecy if I can't even beat my own brother in a fight?"

Cassie chuckled, "It's not so ancient a prophecy as you might imagine . . . " After a pause, she said, "Physical strength can be gained with hard work and repetition. Combat skills can be learned. What is impossible is to teach a stupid man to be an intellectual."

"That's what people go to school for," he said, confused, "Knowledge can always be taught."

"Knowledge, yes, but not wisdom. An ignorant man needs only knowledge to lose his ignorance. A stupid man gains knowledge, yet has not the wisdom to use it."

Bridgot was silent, contemplating.

"You're not stupid," Cassie said, "You have the brains to succeed on this quest in ways the simple farm boys of this village could never hope to. When something goes wrong, you'll figure out how to keep going. You're a critical thinker, and a problem solver. Strength and skill with a weapon are not what make a warrior great. Brute strength is not enough to keep you alive on its own. It's your mind. Why do you think the warrior of the prophecy had to be the one who could solve the riddle?"

"Thank you," he replied, giving her a smile.

"Of course, dear," she said, "Now, go and make me proud."

As the vision faded away, and Vega came back to her handshake with King Boreas of Ivonneveille, the two men were staring at her, anxiously awaiting what she would say. "I have to go," she said suddenly, "It was a pleasure meeting you."

"What did you see?" Kamine's father asked, "What was your vision?"

"I'm not sure yet," she replied, "It was quite far in the future. I don't even know how it's relevant to either of you. Only time will tell. Now, if you'll excuse me, I'd like to talk to your daughter before we leave tomorrow."

Vega ran all the way to the Tree of Knowledge, trying to piece together what she'd seen. It was beginning to grow dark, and she was worried she wouldn't find Kamine in time to say goodbye. Just then, she felt a buzzing in her apron pocket. She pulled out the mirror Jezebelle had given her, and saw her face in it.

"Vega?" she said, "Where are you?"

"I'm at the Tree of Knowledge," she replied, "I'm trying to find Kamine."

"Another star has formed," Jezebelle said.

Vega's eyes widened, "I just had a vision." After a pause, she said, "What can this mean?"

"I'm not sure," she responded, "We'll just have to piece your visions together to figure it out."

She nodded, catching the reflection of her brown eyes over the image of Jezebelle. From the top of her field of vision, something moved. She looked up, and there was Kamine, seated beside the Tree, leaning against its trunk.

"I have to go," Vega said, "We can discuss this upon my return tonight. Fughar and I are leaving in the morning."

"Very well," Jezebelle replied, "Tell her hello for me."

Before she could respond, the silver-haired librarian vanished from the mirror's surface. She tucked it back in her apron pocket, walking over to Kamine.

"What are you doing here?" the young elf girl asked.

"I came to find you," she replied.

She didn't respond.

Vega sighed, "I'm sorry, Kamine. For everything. It was never my intention to take your father from you. If it were up to me, he would stay here with you all the time. But, my visions rule. I just wish I understood what they mean." After a pause, she said, "Anyway, I just wanted to say I'm sorry, and I wanted to say goodbye." She turned to walk away.

"Wait," Kamine said.

She turned around.

"I forgive you. I know you wouldn't do anything to hurt me. You're my friend. I know it must be important, or you wouldn't ask. It's just . . . "

"You don't want your father to go."

She nodded, "Anyway, I don't want you to leave on bad terms. Come, sit with me."

Vega walked over to the Tree to sit beside Kamine. As she placed her hand against its trunk to gain the leverage to sit, something happened. She felt the glowing pulses from the Tree running through her. She couldn't explain the sensation. It was warm, it was ancient, it was tingly, it was powerful enough to knock her over. It made her experience joy, pain, anger, sadness, fear, love, and every other possible feeling all at once.

Suddenly, she understood things. Grown-up things. Things she never thought she would understand. But, most importantly, she understood her visions. She understood how they worked, how they were related, what they meant. She knew that the things she'd seen were never guaranteed. The current path they were on would lead them there, but the slightest variation could change the course of destiny forever. Then, the Tree gave her a vision. She saw the dark wizard, Nazirdok—the one who had killed Irvenix. He was conducting a ritual. As the stars aligned overhead, it was complete. Dark forces penetrated his body, and he was transformed. With malice in his eyes and in his heart, he strode from the palace, killing the dwarven and elven armies, which had assembled to fight his troops. It took only a wave for him to destroy an entire army. He moved through the land, killing at will. His reign of darkness spread, and no one could challenge him.

One hundred years passed, and finally, there was one who could defeat him. He had grown old and weak, and could not wield his power on the same level he once did. She saw the people he killed—each and every one. Over that long a period, there weren't many good people left in the world. The pain, suffering, and death he caused before his defeat was immeasurable.

No, Vega thought, *There must be a way to stop him from completing that ritual . . .*

As soon as she'd thought it, she once again saw Princess Celestia—the woman from her earlier vision. She realized that meant she could stop him. Suddenly, it all made sense. The Great Prophecy must be about her, stopping Nazirdok. Bridgot and Aurano were meant to help her also. But, she remembered what Celestia had said about a dwarf, and she knew she didn't yet have all the pieces to this puzzle.

Then, it hit her. *That's why I need to go to the land of the dwarves,* she thought, *I don't know yet why Boreas and Boreas need to come with me, but I have a feeling their part in this is yet to be revealed.*

With purpose, the Tree of Knowledge launched her back, wisdom and light filling her body to its max. The overload had made her headache reach its peak, and the unbearable pain caused her to lose consciousness . . .

"Vega! Vega!" Kamine shouted with worry.

Her head was still throbbing as she regained consciousness. She realized she was no longer beside the Tree of Knowledge. She was back at the library, with Fughar standing over her. Kamine and Jezebelle were close by.

They all gasped as she opened her eyes. They stepped back, staring at her uncertainly.

"What?" she asked, "What is it?"

"Your eyes," Jezebelle said breathlessly.

"My eyes?" she said, panicking, "What's wrong with them?"

"Look," Fughar said, holding up a mirror.

Vega stared into it, disbelieving what she was seeing. Her eyes were glowing white, with no pupil or iris. The familiar human brown was gone, leaving behind these haunting orbs. "What happened?" she cried, pushing the mirror away.

"Can you see?" Fughar asked.

"Yes!" she shouted, "What's wrong with them?" Tears of panic began to stream down her cheeks.

"It was the Tree," Kamine said, "It had to be!"

"Yes, it was the Tree," Jezebelle agreed, "It has chosen you. You aren't just any old oracle. You are The Oracle. You're the greatest of them all. The Tree of Knowledge doesn't choose just anyone to share its light with. What did it show you?"

Her face was soaked with tears, now, "It showed me another piece of the puzzle. There will be a Great Prophecy that I must share with the world. But, I cannot share it in pieces. When that row of stars is done forming, I shall know."

Jezebelle nodded, understanding.

"The Tree shared knowledge and wisdom with me. Now, I understand my visions. I know things I never thought I would. I know what it means to be an oracle."

The three of them stood solemnly, bowing their heads to her in awe.

After a long pause, Kamine stepped forward, "Take my father with you. If that is what you have foreseen, then that is how it must be. The very Tree of Knowledge has deemed you worthy. Who am I to disagree?" She paused again, "You are my friend. You always will be."

Vega teared up again as she hopped off the table they had laid her on, hugging Kamine, "Thank you. I will always hold you in my heart as my friend, too."

"Are you still up to traveling?" Fughar asked, "Or shall I postpone our departure?"

"No," Vega answered, "We leave at dawn."

Dirthix

7

When morning came, Fughar and Vega met up with the Boreases by the horse corral. Fughar's red mare, Sage was waiting for them, saddled and ready. Elf Boreas had his white stallion, Breeze, and human Boreas had his black stallion, Phoenix.

"Ready to set out, young oracle?" Boreas asked. He faltered when he caught sight of her eyes, his own widening, "What in the world?"

"Your Tree of Knowledge has chosen her," Fughar said, "imparting its light and wisdom within her. She is now The Oracle."

"That is spooky," King Boreas said, scratching his brown beard.

Boreas swallowed, his black hair standing on end, his dark skin covered with goosebumps. After a pause, he said, "Very well. Let's set out."

The Boreases traveled upon their horses uneasily, keeping a watchful eye upon Vega the whole while. She sat behind Fughar upon Sage's back, lost in her own thoughts as they traversed the elven forest, *What pieces are left of this puzzle? What will we find in the land of the dwarves?*

When they stopped to make camp, the four of them sat around a small fire, loading up on elven breads and fruits. The forest was aglow with life around them, and Vega had a deep understanding of this place, and all the creatures within it, after her experience with the Tree.

"So, Boreas and Boreas?" Fughar said, "We need a better way to differentiate the two of you."

"Well, he's a king, and I'm not," Boreas replied.

"Still," Vega inserted, "It's not very concise to call him King Boreas all the time."

"You can call me B," King Boreas said, "Humans aren't so formal as elves. I don't mind a nickname." He chuckled, "My brothers all call me B."

"Excellent," Fughar replied, "Boreas and B."

The three men began chatting, and Vega wandered into the forest. As soon as she'd reached the treeline, she came upon a nymph. The beautiful forest guardian with cloud-like hair and viny apparel backed away, fearful of her.

"It's alright," she said, "I won't hurt you. I'm an oracle. I was chosen by the Tree of Knowledge. Would you like me to view your future?"

The nymph looked at her curiously, inching closer.

Vega smiled, "Hold out your hand."

She did so, her glistening skin sparkling in the moonlight.

She grabbed her hand, tuning into the energy the Tree had granted her to fuel her visions. With the magic of the elven forest inside her, she could control her visions more, viewing things at will. Though, she would never be able to control them completely, as certain things were meant for her to see, and certain things were not.

She was standing in the elven forest, and she could see the very same nymph before her. She began to wonder whether she was actually having a vision, or whether she had simply opened her eyes. The forest was green and vibrant, and she realized all the nymph wanted to see was that she would be successful in her endeavor to keep the trees alive and healthy. And, indeed, it appeared she would.

Vega smiled as she returned to the present, releasing her arm, "Your forest shall stay alive and healthy, indeed."

The nymph beamed, obviously happy. She took Vega's arm, leading her further into the forest. She brought her to a clearing. Several other nymphs were gathered there. They looked up, angry and fearful as they saw her entering their clearing. The one guiding her calmed them, obviously communicating with her fellow nymphs. They pulled Vega to the center of the clearing, and placed their hands upon her. Suddenly, she felt their collective consciousness as their soft, gentle energy passed into her.

Without having to wonder, Vega knew what had happened. They had granted her a small portion of magic, which could be used by her to perform a single spell. It was a gift from them, to thank her for her vision. "Thank you," she said, "I will cherish this gift."

They nodded, and the first nymph helped her up, guiding her back to her campsite.

"Where have you been?" Fughar demanded, "You can't just go wandering off on your own."

"I have been granted a gift by the nymphs," she replied, "in exchange for my vision of the future of this forest."

The three men looked at her in shock and wonder, wordless.

"I'd hoped a pixie would grant me a wish, but this is good, too. It will come in handy, I think."

They continued to stare at her silently.

She felt their eyes boring into her, and the awkwardness caught up with her, "Well, goodnight, gentlemen."

"Goodnight, Vega," Fughar said quickly, snapping out of it.

"Uh . . . right. I'll take the first watch," B added, as the rest of them settled down to sleep.

The next day was long, slow, and a bit awkward, no one really saying anything. When they stopped to make camp, Vega stepped away again, not sure what to say to these men. She sat apart, at the edge of the forest, feeling alone. Every friend she'd made in her life, she'd had to say goodbye to. Now, she was a freak with glowing eyes. Everyone was afraid of her. She sighed, curling her knees to her chest.

As she sat there, a pixie flew up to her. She gave off a beautiful, ivory light. She landed on Vega's knee, looking as though she were sympathetic to her feelings.

She could see her tiny body, her hair tied up in a miniature bun, her wings flitting behind her. "Hi there, little pixie," she said, giving her a half-smile.

She placed her tiny hands upon her arm, gently, giving her a look of encouragement.

"You're not afraid of my eyes?" she asked.

The pixie shook her head.

Vega smiled, "That's a first."

She smiled back, flapping her wings contentedly.

She held out her finger, and the pixie flew over, landing upon it. "You're a beautiful little pixie, aren't you?"

She twirled happily, her ivory cheeks tinting pink.

"I shall call you . . . Bella."

She gagged in disgust, indicating she didn't care for the name.

"Okay, how about . . . Luna?"

She shook her head, crossing her arms with pride.

"You're right," she said, "It's too obvious for a pixie."

She nodded, ivory light burning brightly.

She sighed, "I'm not very good at this, am I?" After a pause, she said, "What about . . . Tabatha?"

The pixie began twirling again, beaming happily.

"You like it, huh?" she asked, smiling, "Very well. Tabatha, it is."

"Thanks for sitting with me," Vega said, "It's nice to have a friend."

She smiled at her, flitting over and sitting on her knee.

They stayed like that for a while, before Vega decided it was time to return to the fire. Tabatha seemed upset when she got up to walk away, flying after her.

"I'm sorry," she said, "I have to go."

She stubbornly flew after her.

"I'm afraid you can't come with me," Vega said, "We're leaving the elven forest."

Tabatha continued to follow her, sticking close by her side.

"Looks like you've got an admirer," Boreas said.

"Yes," she replied, "But, what can I do? She can't come with us . . . can she?"

"That's up to her," he replied, "I guess we'll find out when we leave the forest tomorrow, whether she's still willing to follow."

The pixie landed upon her shoulder, sitting with the rest of them by the fire. She seemed content to stay by Vega's side. *I guess he's right,* she thought, *We'll see tomorrow . . .*

As they set out on horseback for the land of the dwarves, the pixie sat upon Vega's shoulder while they rode. She hadn't expected her to come along, but it seemed she wished to accompany her. They rode all day—out of the ancient forest of the elves, and into the green and brown forest of Korga. Tabatha remained on her shoulder as they crossed the border. Vega smiled, glad to have some company on her travels.

They were met by a line of dwarves on ponies. They led them to the dwarven tunnels, taking them inside. Breeze, Phoenix, and Sage were led to the stables, as they were taken to the palace. Fughar appeared nervous, his frail body covered with goosebumps. Boreas looked on edge, his pointed ears perked. B appeared confident, as a king should. Tabatha seemed a bit uneasy, hiding in Vega's gold and amber hair.

They entered the massive throne room of the dwarf king, its empty spaces covered in gold and jewels. Vega had read about the dwarven tunnels, but seeing them in person was very different, just like her experience in the land of the elves. The tall, intricately carved, bejeweled structure was breathtaking.

"What brings humans and an elf to the land of the dwarves?" the king asked, rising from his throne. He had tan skin, tarnished with dirt, a dirty-blonde beard, and he was garbed in a miner's uniform with a golden crown upon his head. She was surprised to see a king who obviously worked alongside his people.

They all looked to Vega for an answer. She swallowed, unsure what to say. How could she tell the dwarf king she didn't know why they were there? He would certainly not understand the magical forces that propelled them there.

"She is The Oracle," Boreas said finally, much to her relief, "She had a vision that we were supposed to come here. We do not yet understand why, but I am quite sure it shall be revealed very soon."

"Sire," Fughar said, "If I may . . . "

"Drewg," the king interjected, "That is my name. King Drewg of Dirthix."

Fughar bowed respectfully, "King Drewg, if I may, we only seek accommodations for a short while. Once we know the meaning of her vision, we will know what to do next. We'll be out of your hair as soon as we can."

He scratched his scruffy beard, nodding, "Very well. Torvus and Krater will show you to your rooms. Inform them as soon as you have your answer."

They bowed in agreement as two red-bearded dwarves entered, leading them from the throne room. They followed them to two suites situated in the corridor. The massive beds within were able to come apart. They watched in amazement as Torvus and Krater separated them, providing each room with two beds. Boreas and B entered one, situating themselves. Fughar and Vega entered the other.

The old medicine man spread his quilt over his bed, placing herbs and incense on the bedside table. Vega was amazed by his ability to make anywhere home. She wished she could do the same, because every unfamiliar place was difficult for her. She missed her house, and her parents. She sat on the edge of the bed she'd been provided, wishing there was a window she could look out of.

Tabatha came out of her hair finally, sitting upon her shoulder once more. The little ivory pixie was her only comfort as she traveled. She was grateful for her company, feeling her slight weight on her shoulder. She held out her finger, and she landed upon it. "I'm glad you decided to stick around, Tabatha," she said.

"Tabatha?" Fughar asked.

"Yes," Vega replied, "That's what I named her."

The old man smiled, shaking his head.

Just then, Krater came to the door, inviting them to come and eat with them. "You came on a good night," he said, "Our people are holding a feast in honor of our newest warrior, Kgandor."

They met up with Torvus, who was leading Boreas and B. They all ventured into the Great Hall, where the food was being served. There were a few open seats at a table in the midst of all the rowdy, celebrating dwarves. There were heaps of meats, cheeses, and breads brought forth, as glasses of mead were passed around to all the adults. The children were given a strange liquid Vega had never seen before.

"What is it?" she asked.

"It's meaj," Krater said, "It's made from wheat, like the mead, but it's not fermented."

Vega took a sip. It tasted nutty and subtle. It wasn't bad. It couldn't compare to the juices of the elves, but it was better than she expected.

"What do you think?" Torvus asked eagerly.

"It's good," she replied, "It's surprisingly good."

The two red-bearded dwarves smiled, going back to their plates.

"I've never been to Korga before," B said, holding his crown so the dancing dwarves wouldn't knock it off.

"Neither have I," Boreas said, looking as though that had been a plus.

As they ate, they could see a red-bearded dwarf being lifted up by the other dwarves. "Is that Kgandor?" Vega asked.

Krater nodded.

Something in her knew she needed to talk to him—that he was the key to her next vision. "I want to meet him," she said.

Torvus and Krater looked at her questioningly.

"To congratulate him," she added quickly.

They smiled. "Of course," Torvus said.

"Becoming a dwarven warrior is a huge accomplishment!" Krater added.

The two of them led her over to his table, ducking and dodging the celebrating dwarves.

"Kgandor!" Torvus called.

"This young oracle would like to congratulate you!" Krater said.

The other dwarves suddenly set him down in front of her with a *thud!*

"Well, hello, young lady!" he said, looking at her.

Vega gave him a nod, "Hello, sir. It's a pleasure to meet a dwarven warrior." She extended her hand for him to shake, ready for a vision.

Instead of shaking her hand, the drunken warrior scooped her up, hugging her. As he squeezed her tight, the vision began. She was in the throne room of the dwarf king, but it wasn't Drewg on the throne. It was a blonde-bearded man garbed in gold, with a too-long cape and a too-tall crown. As she watched, a red-bearded dwarf who looked very much like Kgandor entered.

"Kgansten!" the king called, "My dear nephew!"

"Hello, Uncle Thanghor," Kgansten said, drawing near.

"I have good news for you, nephew," he said, "I know you wish to do what your father—my brother—couldn't, and become a Dwarf Lord. I must say, you are well on your way. But, there is a quest to be embarked upon. The princess of The Great Prophecy has been discovered. She is on her way here, along with her human and elven warriors. They will require a dwarven warrior to accompany them. Success on a quest of such importance would guarantee you the title."

"Are you saying I have a shot at becoming that warrior?" Kgansten asked eagerly.

"I'm saying you *are* that warrior," King Thanghor replied, "If you want to be. I am appointing you the honor."

"Oh, wow, Uncle Thanghor," he said, "You have no idea how much this means to me!"

"I think I do," he said, "The line of Kgandor deserves to finally gain the title he worked so hard for . . . the title he sacrificed his life for."

The vision faded away as he set her back on the ground, going back to the party. Torvus and Krater ushered her away quickly, as she processed what she'd seen. So, his son would become the dwarven warrior of her prophecy. And, this warrior she'd just met would die trying to become a Dwarf Lord . . .

"You seemed out of sorts after you met the dwarven warrior," Fughar said, once they'd returned to their room, "You had a vision, didn't you?"

She nodded, "I know what I need to know now."

"Does that mean it is time for us to leave?"

"I'm not sure yet," she replied, "I want to stay at least a couple more days."

"Very well," he said, "Goodnight, Vega."

As soon as he'd said it, the witch's glass in her pocket began buzzing. She answered it, looking at Jezebelle's face, "A star formed, didn't it?"

The elf-witch nodded, "Yes. You had a vision, I take it?"

It was Vega's turn to nod, "Yes."

Jezebelle was silent, contemplating.

"How many more stars are left to form?"

"Three," she answered, "Four have formed already, for a total of seven."

"Four?" she said, "I thought there were only three that had formed."

"One formed after your vision through the Tree of Knowledge," she replied, "I didn't have the chance to tell you."

Vega nodded in understanding, "What pieces can there be left of this puzzle?"

"I'm afraid I cannot help you to form the complete picture of your visions. I can only tell you what I've observed."

"Thank you," she said, "Everything helps. It feels that this prophecy is too great for me to be the one to prophesy it. Yet, I know that I am."

"You shall be great," Jezebelle replied.

She sighed, still unsure, "Keep me up to date."

The silver-haired elf nodded as her image faded away.

"Well, Tabatha," Vega said, holding out her finger for her pixie friend to land upon, "We've got work to do."

The tiny pixie did a little spin, sparkling dust flying around her.

The next day, Vega moved slowly, unsure what it would hold. She felt it wasn't time to leave Korga, but she didn't yet know why. Her visions disturbed her; the images they displayed often plaguing her dreams. Cassie being attacked, then Miss Geneva . . . how scant Cassie looked in her vision of the drought . . . young Arenelle being killed . . . knowing Irvenix and Kgandor would die as well . . . not to mention all the death and destruction left in Nazirdok's wake . . . it was enough to drive her mad.

As she was meandering a corridor of the dwarven tunnels, she heard voices. She paused, unsure if she should round the corner.

"One day, you'll be king, Thanghor. Then, you can make the rules. But until then, you must do as Drewg says."

"I know, Kgandor," he replied, "I just don't want to live in my father's shadow. I want to be my own man—my own king. I don't want the people to compare me to him."

"I don't think there's any avoiding that," Kgandor said, "They compare every king to the one before."

Thanghor sighed, "You're lucky. People don't compare you to your father. You have the freedom to be your own man. Last night, people celebrated you for becoming a dwarven warrior. Not one word was spoken about your father."

"I took a different path from my father. He's a miner. I'm a warrior. If I followed in his footsteps, people would compare me to him, too."

"I suppose you're right," he said, "What would I do without you?"

Kgandor laughed, "I'm not sure. I suppose it's a good thing I married your sister!"

"But you were too proud to take her title," he chided.

"I don't want to become a noble by marriage. I want to *earn* my place as a Dwarf Lord."

"Well, you'll always be a brother to me," Thanghor said.

"As will you," he replied, "But, don't go getting all sentimental on me! Come on, let's go find something to eat!"

Vega scurried back down the corridor, not wanting them to think she was intentionally eavesdropping. As much as she wanted to prevent his death, a realization hit her: if she did, Kgansten would not become the warrior of the prophecy. Without him, they would not succeed against Nazirdok. Everything happened for a reason. And, each piece of the puzzle had to happen the way it was destined to, or it would crumble.

With the knowledge and wisdom the Tree had shared with her, came the greatest burden of bearing it. She had to allow some small tragedies to avoid larger ones. Her visions weren't always meant to help. Some would only ever bring her pain. Tabatha patted her cheek as she felt her distress, balancing precariously on her shoulder.

Vega let a few tears roll down her cheek as she slumped against an elaborately carved wall in the dwarven tunnels. *Now, it's time to go,* she thought.

Byun

8

When morning came, the four of them set out through the dwarven tunnels upon their steeds. Vega sat behind Fughar with Tabatha on her shoulder. The Boreases rode their horses beside them as they made their way out of Dirthix.

With three more stars to form, Vega knew it meant she would have three more visions related to the prophecy. The four she'd had already had been of Aurano becoming the elven warrior, Princess Celestia and Bridgot referring to the fulfilled prophecy, Nazirdok's rise to power should he succeed, and Kgansten becoming the dwarven warrior. She knew not what her three remaining visions would hold, but she knew they were vital to her prophecy.

It was becoming hard for her to be a kid, with everything she'd seen. The knowledge the Tree had given her had advanced her understanding of the world beyond her years. The pain and suffering she'd witnessed were enough to zap the innocence right out of her. She couldn't see herself as a child anymore, though others still would.

She wasn't sure where they were headed—only that it was time for them to leave Korga. She knew she needed to find a place to call home, where she could be safe and free to use her powers the way she chose, not the way others would use them. She had no idea where that would be. She knew she couldn't stay with her parents in Kataran, nor with the elves or dwarves.

Wherever she wound up needed to be safe and secluded, so no one could try to use her powers to their own ends. She began to realize she would need a better keeper than Fughar. Though he could care for her well enough, and he cared about her, he was not strong enough to protect her. He was a frail old medicine man. She needed a warrior.

After about a week in the dwarven tunnels, their saddlebags began to deplete. They decided to stop in one of the dwarven villages to refill their supplies. None of them knew dwarvish, so it was difficult for them to communicate, as that was the only language most of the dwarven citizens knew. Finally, a young dwarven man with golden skin, black hair, a black beard, and narrow eyes approached them at one of the inns.

"I speak human," he said, "I can translate."

"We would be humbly obliged," B said, nodding to him.

He turned to the innkeepers, "Brathnas, siestras, yaug es frugs. Yaug iskeet jhutz. Sie vrada hilgite. Du gnozims fu on neet."

"Du gnozims?" one of them replied, "Aye, sie konder hilgite. Zaug kguys."

"Follow her," the dwarf said, "She will show you to your rooms."

"Thank you," Fughar said, "We appreciate the help."

He gave them a nod, as they followed the innkeeper up the short stairs and to two rooms. "Zaug," she said, gesturing to the two rooms, "Du gnozims fu on neet."

"Jdaren," Boreas said, nodding.

They looked at him.

"What?" he said, "It means, 'thank you.' I know a few dwarvish phrases—not enough to communicate effectively."

The blonde innkeeper smiled, turning and making her way down the stairs.

"Let's just get settled in for the night," B said, going into one of the rooms. Boreas followed, leaving Vega to room with Fughar again.

The room was small, and Vega made her bed on the floor, since Fughar was too old to climb down there and get back up. Her tiny pixie friend made her bed on one of the bedposts, curling up with a small patch of a blanket Vega had cut for her.

The floor was dusty and creaky, but she made the best of it, cocooning herself with blankets and pillows. As she drifted off, a vision floated through her mind. She was at a royal human party. There were people all around, garbed in ballgowns and royal robes. An unfamiliar king and queen sat upon the thrones. Near the punch bowl, she saw three princesses chatting. Well, two of them were chatting excitedly, while the third seemed in her own world.

"I hope he dances with me!" one of them squealed, "Wouldn't that be exquisite!" She had red hair, freckles, and a pink ballgown.

"He's so gorgeous," the second one said breathlessly, "I just wish he would notice me." She sighed, staring longingly toward the top of the stairs. She had brown hair and a green ballgown.

"What about you, Eva?" the first one asked, seeming annoyed.

"Yeah," the second one chimed in, "You've hardly said a word tonight."

The third princess had light brown skin, caramel hair, and deep brown eyes. She wore a lavender ballgown, and a blank expression. She blinked, seeming to snap back to reality, and looked back and forth between her friends, "I . . . uh . . . I don't really know what to think of him. I've never heard of him before." She paused, seeming flustered, "Truth be told, I've been to so many coming out parties this year, I don't even remember whose this one is."

The first girl scoffed, "Never heard of him? He's only the most eligible bachelor in all the land."

The second girl looked at her more sympathetically, "This is Prince Ladon's party. The one . . . the only." She sighed again.

Eva looked unsure, brushing her fingers through her hair nervously. Vega thought she looked familiar, but at first, she couldn't place it. Finally, she realized that this was the queen she'd seen from one of her other visions. She was Princess Celestia's mother!

Just then, the doors at the top of the stairs opened, and the announcer bellowed, "Presenting Prince Ladon of Tristétoiless!"

A young man with pale skin, brown hair, blue eyes, and a short brown beard descended the stairs. He wore red royal robes and a crown upon his head. As he made his way down to his party, his eyes locked in on a certain spot, and he seemingly couldn't look away. Everyone moved out of his path, whispering to each other, and trying to determine what—or who—he was looking at.

As they watched, he made his way straight over to Princess Eva. She was staring at him as well, their eyes linked. Her two friends were wide-eyed with jealous surprise, gawking as he offered her his hand for a dance. She accepted, and they spun onto the dance floor, never taking their eyes off each other.

The king and queen seemed thrilled, watching the two of them. Vega guessed it was because the merging of their kingdoms would mean greater territory for their descendants. And, as she knew from previous visions, that's exactly what would happen. As she watched, her vision shifted, and she was in a corridor of portraits. Prince Ladon and Princess Eva were there.

"I always knew my brother would abdicate. He never wanted the throne. Everyone always thought I'd make a better king. Yet, now that it's actually happened, I'm not sure I will," Ladon sighed. "Look at all of them," he nodded toward the portraits along the wall, "Generations of my family. They've made this kingdom prosper for centuries. I'm just not sure I'll ever measure up."

"You will," Eva said, touching his arm, "I know it."

He looked at her.

"No one cares more about their people than you. You do what's best for them, and put them first. That's what a great king does," she smiled. After a pause, she sighed, looking away, "Not like me. I don't have what it takes. But, I'm my kingdom's only option. I can't abdicate like your brother. I have no siblings." She paused again, "It's not fair."

Ladon looked at her, "Life's not fair . . . not for anyone. But I ask you, who better? Who is better suited to rule than us? Who else trains their whole lives for the job? It may not be fair we were born royal while others were not, but we are the only ones qualified to rule. No one else could handle it. No one else understands the rigor, the responsibility, the sacrifice. They see only the luxury, the wealth, the power. We understand that it's more than that. *You* understand that it's more than that. That is why you'll make a great queen. Not because of your royal blood, but because of your knowledge, wisdom, and caring heart."

Eva smiled, "You always know just what to say. It's just another reason you'll make a great king. But, you won't be like any of your predecessors."

He looked at her in surprise.

"You'll be better," she finished, smiling coyly.

Ladon smiled, taking her hands in his and kissing them, "What would I do without you?"

Vega's vision changed again, and she saw the two of them in the throne room, smiling. Eva was holding a baby in her arms. The two of them had larger crowns upon their heads, and she realized they were king and queen now.

"Milady," a servant said, bowing, "The people have come bearing gifts for your daughter."

"Not all of them could attend her presentation," Ladon said, putting his arm around his wife, "Send them in."

They were glowing as the people brought gifts before them, placing them at their feet. "This is all for you," Eva said, kissing her daughter's forehead, "My sweet Celestia."

Just then, a servant burst in, "Sire! Forgive my intrusion, but the sentinels have informed me that the armies of Kiteau are marching on our gate!"

King Ladon straightened up, looking determined, "Ready the troops."

The people began to panic, running from the room.

"Everyone!" he announced, "Please, remain calm. Return to your homes in an orderly fashion. We will protect our kingdom, and our people."

They moved more slowly from the room, still in obvious panic.

Queen Eva stood frozen, clutching their daughter to her chest. Finally, she broke her silence, handing the baby off to a servant, "Ladon, I know you hold steadfast to your duties, but just stop and think. We have a daughter now. We're a family. We need you. We could just step down, retire, become nobles. You wouldn't have to fight!"

"And leave our people to fend for themselves?" he shouted, "Leave our kingdom up for grabs? Who's to stop Kiteau from taking over? I will not be a coward! I will not abandon my people when they need me the most!"

"But, you will abandon our family?" she cried, "What if something happens to you?"

"Then you will rule in my place," he said solemnly.

"No," she said, "I refuse. I will not remain on this throne without you. I didn't even want to be queen! I can't lose you!"

"I will say no more," he said, unable to look at her, "I will do my duty as king."

She ran from the room, bursting into tears as soon as she reached the hallway. Vega watched it change again. This time, they were outside. Eva was walking toward her. She was wearing all black, with a veil over her face. Vega's breath caught as she turned to see a coffin of stone. It had a sculpture of Ladon lying upon it.

Eva stood alone, placing her trembling hands upon it, and sobbing softly. "Why?" she said suddenly, "Why did you take him from me?"

Vega's vision faded away, and she awoke, eyes scanning the small, dusty room of the dwarven inn. She sighed solemnly, taking in what she'd seen.

The next morning, as they were eating breakfast, the golden-skinned dwarf with narrow eyes approached them. "Good morning, all of you. Were you accommodated sufficiently?"

"Yes, thank you," Fughar replied, "I'm relieved you could translate for us."

"Aye," he said, "I *can* translate for you."

B shot him a questioning look, "What do you mean by that?"

"I mean that the four of you are traveling through dwarven territory, but none of you speak dwarvish. You'll need to stop in villages along the way through the tunnels to refill your supplies. How do you intend to do that on your own? You were lucky I came along here. You need me."

"Are you saying you'd like to accompany us?" Fughar asked.

The dwarf nodded.

"No," Boreas said, "No way. I'm sorry, but I'm not traveling with a dwarf."

"But, he can help us," B said, "Be reasonable. I know there is a feud of dwarves and elves, but this is more important."

"I'm not so childish and naive as to sacrifice our mission for sake of a feud," he retorted, "I don't trust outsiders to know our business. We don't even know what his intentions are."

"Then, let's find out," B said, turning to the dwarf, "Why would you want to accompany us?"

"If I tell you the truth, you're likely to laugh in my face," he said, "But, I shall tell you anyway. I'm bored. I sit in this village day in and day out with nothing to do. I was forcibly retired due to a back injury. I can't do manual labor anymore. No woman will have me. No one wants a man who can't work." He sighed, looking away, "I just want to get out of here. I don't really care where you're going, or what your mission is."

After a long pause, Boreas said, "Very well. We are in need of a translator. But, if you do *anything* suspicious, I will not hesitate to kill you, dwarf."

He nodded eagerly.

"What is your name?"

"Byun," he replied, standing straight.

"Nice to meet you, Byun," Vega said, breaking the tension, "I'm Vega."

"The pleasure is all mine, young one," he said, smiling.

"This is Fughar," she said, "And, this is Boreas and Boreas."

He stared at the dark elf and the brown-bearded human king questioningly.

"Confusing, I know," she said, gesturing to the human, "We call this one B."

"Well, Byun," Boreas said sharply, "We must be off. Do you have a horse?"

"I have a dwarven pony," he replied, "She's a beauty. Her name is Kimmi."

"Well, get her," he snapped, "Let's go."

When the black-bearded dwarf vanished, B said, "You don't have to be so harsh with him."

"Yes," Fughar agreed, "*He's* doing *us* a favor."

As the four of them mounted their steeds, Byun came riding up on a red pony. "Told you she was a beauty," he said, patting her.

"Yes, she is," Vega said from behind Fughar, shooting him a smile.

Boreas shook his reins, setting out through the tunnels. Everyone else shook their heads, following him.

It was very quiet the next couple days, as they continued through the dwarven tunnels with their newfound companion. The tension between Byun and Boreas was tangible, and it made the rest of them uncomfortable. Vega could feel Tabatha's nerves as she hid beneath her hair.

The tunnels of the dwarves seemed to go on forever, and Vega wasn't sure how much longer they would have to continue before they saw the sun. They stopped in another village, Byun translating for them with the innkeeper. They were able to get three rooms this time, but Vega was still made to share with Fughar, as he was her keeper, and she was considered too young and vulnerable to have a room to herself.

As she fell asleep curled up on the floor, she thought, *Will I ever find a place to call home? And why were the Boreases supposed to accompany me? When will the rest of these visions come to me?*

As they set out again, Boreas said, "We should reach the end of the tunnels in three more days. Where do we go from there, Vega?"

B, Fughar, and Byun all turned to look at her. She grew nervous, unsure what to say. She knew that Kogatsa was not where she belonged. But, she also knew that was where Nazirdok would conduct his ritual. She thought it could induce another vision. On the other hand, she didn't think there was much more she needed to see concerning him, or that she would want to see it. She began to think that west was the way to go.

Before she could open her mouth to answer, however, they heard a loud, low grumble. Heavy footsteps echoed through the corridor. The five of them stopped in their tracks. The Boreases armed themselves quickly. Byun followed suit, lifting his axe from its place on his pony. Fughar steadied his red mare, Sage, preparing to run at a moment's notice to protect Vega.

Boreas' white stallion, Breeze, and B's black stallion, Phoenix, bristled nervously. Byun's red pony, Kimmi, was calm and steady. She was obviously trained for war. As the footsteps neared, even she grew nervous, however.

As they watched, a massive troll made its way around the corner. Vega's eyes grew wide at the sight. It towered above them—grayish-brown skin, garbed in a loincloth, and covered in growths. It was huge and grotesque to behold. It caught sight of them, tongue flicking out of its mouth as it licked its lips. It began coming toward them, raising a massive club over its head.

The Boreases rode out to meet it, firing a stream of arrows at it. Byun followed behind, raising his axe. The arrows had little to no effect, and they finally drew their swords as they neared the creature, ready to put up a fight.

The troll began swinging its club, bringing it down on various parts of the floor as it attempted to crush them. The Boreases maneuvered their horses quickly, avoiding the attack. They were obviously struggling to stay out of the way and actually do some damage.

As she watched, Vega realized she couldn't see Byun anywhere. The Boreases were fighting this troll alone. She knew it wouldn't be long before Fughar rode the two of them to safety, abandoning their friends in an effort to keep her safe.

Suddenly, the troll bellowed in pain, and they all stopped and stared as they saw Byun upon its back, axe protruding from its head. It stumbled forward, collapsing to the marble floor in front of them. They all stared in awe, the Boreases dumbfounded.

"You just have to know how to deal with the creature before you," Byun said, leaping to the floor from the troll's back. He clambered back up, realizing he'd forgotten his axe, and yanked it from the creature's head, wiping it clean.

Fughar nearly fainted at the sight. Vega grimaced, feeling nauseous. Boreas stared at him in shock, unsure what to say.

"That was amazing!" B shouted, "Well done, Byun! I, for one, am glad we have you."

"Thank you," he replied, bowing, "It was an honor to be of service."

"I thought you couldn't do anything due to your back," Boreas said.

"I can't do any heavy lifting," he replied, "And I must take it easy in combat. But, a cave troll is no problem for your average dwarf. We're used to them in these tunnels. I can still handle that much."

"Well, thank you," Fughar inserted, "We appreciate you saving our lives."

"Yes," Vega agreed, "You were very brave and knowledgeable."

Byun bowed again, mounting his steed, "Let us continue on. We have only a few days left before we're out of these tunnels."

Gachichken

9

"Boreas!" a woman with blonde hair and blue eyes called, rushing forward to greet B.

"Aura!" he replied, leaping from Phoenix's back. They embraced, him scooping her up in his arms.

"Father!" a young man shouted, running up to them. He was the spitting image of human Boreas, but with his mother's blue eyes.

B set Aura down, embracing the man, "Jon, my son!"

"Daddy!" a young girl squealed, rushing up. She looked like the preteen version of Aura.

B scooped her up next, squeezing her tight, "How's my Lucy?"

"Better, now that you're back," she said happily.

The four of them walked to a castle, going inside. *This must be B's family,* Vega thought, *his home.*

Boreas' son, Jon, daughter, Lucy, and wife, Aura, made their presence known to their servants when they entered. They led B to the throne room, saying they had a surprise.

A young woman with dark skin and raven hair entered the throne room. She wore a crown and a royal purple ballgown. Her brown eyes twinkled uncertainly. Prince Jon walked over to her, putting his arm around her. Aura fiddled with her pink ballgown nervously. Lucy backed behind her mother, brown eyes wide. B looked around at his family members in confusion.

"I'm engaged, father," Jon said finally, "This is my fiancé, Dia."

"Pleasure to meet you, sir," Dia said, nodding.

"Where are you from?" Boreas asked.

She took a breath, "I am from the kingdom of Swogo, in the land of Tomainda."

"Tomainda?" he asked, "I've never heard of it."

"Yes, it's very far from here," Dia replied, "I'm not surprised you haven't."

"I hadn't either," Jon said, "But it's a real place. And, she's a real princess."

"My father is King Fadhili, and my mother, Queen Jata. My older sister, Kanika, is heir to the throne. I have two other sisters as well: Wamuiru, and my younger sister, Bia."

King Boreas nodded, "Why did you travel here?"

"My oldest sister is heir to our throne. My other older sister has her sights set on a rich and powerful king in a neighboring kingdom. She is known for her looks throughout the land, and is sure to marry well. My younger sister is the baby of the family. She will be cared for no matter what. But, as for me, I'm easily overlooked. I don't belong anywhere. I decided to travel, and see the world. It brought me all the way here. I hadn't planned to stay. Then, I met Jon."

"I know she's not from around here," Jon said, "But, she is of royal blood. And, I love her."

Before Vega could hear B's response, the vision shifted, and she saw Jon and Dia as king and queen. They had a daughter. As she watched, she realized that daughter was Eva—Celestia's mother.

So that means . . . Vega thought, *B is Celestia's great-grandfather!*

As she woke from her vision, she finally realized his significance to her. She realized why shaking his hand had induced a vision of Celestia. She would be his descendant!

"Here we are," Byun said, "The end of the dwarven tunnels."

Vega looked around, realizing she was still on Sage's back behind Fughar.

"Where to?" Boreas asked, looking at her, his elf ears twitching as he sat upon Breeze's back.

Vega sighed, realizing the time had come for a decision, "Abyumo." She wasn't sure what had prompted her to say it, but it sounded right coming out of her mouth.

He nodded, his silky black hair falling over his shoulders.

With that, the five of them exited the tunnels, heading west toward Abyumo.

Vega spent her time pondering everything she'd seen. The world around her was much more complex than her young mind could comprehend before. But, since her encounter with the Tree of Knowledge, she understood much more.

On the road, she was used to Fughar keeping to himself—he was a very solitary man—and the Boreases chatting with each other. She spent her time talking to Tabatha, even though she couldn't talk back. Now that Byun had joined them, he came over to sit beside her.

"Is that a pixie?" he asked.

She looked up, Tabatha twirling on her thumb, "Her name is Tabatha."

"Where'd she come from?" he asked in wonder, scratching his long, black hair.

"The land of the elves," she replied, "She decided to join me when we traveled through."

"I've never seen one in person before," he said.

Vega smiled, "I hadn't, either, until we journeyed to Gliken. I'd only seen pictures in my school books."

Byun smiled back at her, then returned his awestruck gaze to Tabatha, "You must be special for one to have chosen you."

"I don't know about that," she replied, "But, I am an oracle."

"Not just an oracle," Fughar inserted, "*The* Oracle, chosen by the Tree of Knowledge."

Byun's eyes widened, "Wow, really?"

"Careful we don't share too much," Boreas said, "It's not the business of a dwarf translator."

"Relax," B said, "He's one of us now."

"Not in my book," he retorted, "I still don't trust him."

"I'm in the process of predicting a great prophecy," Vega said, rolling her eyes, "And finding a safe place to live. There, now you know what we're doing. I, for one, don't believe you'll do us harm."

Byun smiled, "No, young one, I won't."

"Let's just get some rest," Fughar said, seeing that Boreas was about to say something further, "We shall continue our journey tomorrow."

Boreas grumbled, but said nothing further. Everyone lied down to sleep as the scraggly old medicine man took the first watch.

A couple of weeks went by, as they made their way through Gachichken. One night, as they slept, Vega awoke to shouting, and she quickly jumped up, plucking Tabatha from the ground beside her and placing her on her shoulder before she looked around. Byun and the Boreases were battling a few soldiers. She searched for Fughar, but couldn't find him. Then, she looked down and saw that he was dead. The soldiers had slain him.

Her eyes grew wide with horror. "No!" she shouted, sure this was a vision she needed to wake up from. But, as the soldiers turned their attention to her, she realized it was not. She backed away hurriedly, stumbling over the rocks around their campsite.

"Vega!" Byun shouted, looking over at her worriedly.

The three men fought their way over to her as she tripped, trying to ensure her pixie friend didn't get hurt as she fell. The warriors in her company couldn't get to her fast enough, as a soldier made his way toward her, a dark gleam in his eye that showed his malicious intent. Her eyes grew even wider, tears streaming down as she realized this was her end. The soldier raised his sword, bringing it down upon her.

Before he could land his blow, Tabatha darted out from her hair, pixie dust exploding around her tiny, ivory body. Vega gasped, trying to stop her, but she slipped out of her reach. As the soldier brought his sword down, it hit an invisible barrier, unable to get through. She realized Tabatha's magic had saved her.

Just then, Byun appeared, fighting the soldier back and cutting him down. As the Boreases finished off the rest of them, he held out his hand, "Are you alright?"

Vega nodded, reaching through the barrier so he could help her to her feet. Her little pixie friend released her magic, returning to her shoulder.

"We need to keep moving," B said, "It's unsafe for us here."

Boreas loomed over the two of them, and Vega waited for him to say something to their dwarf friend again. "Not bad, Byun," he said finally, "Thanks for the help."

Byun gave him a nod, and the three of them readied their horses. Vega walked over to Fughar's body, kneeling beside him. "I'm sorry I couldn't foresee *this*," she said, tears streaming down.

B released Fughar's horse, Sage, as Boreas said, "You shall ride with me now, young oracle."

She looked up at him through her tears, "Do you have no heart? Do you not care that he is dead?"

Boreas sighed, softening his tone, "I'm sorry, young one. But, we have no time to dwell here. You must understand that it is not safe. We were ambushed. If we stay, one of us might be next."

"Vega?" Byun said, walking up.

She turned her glowing white eyes on him.

"In light of this tragedy, I would like to offer you my service, as your keeper."

She gave a slight nod, "I will accept, temporarily. I must find someone fit for all aspects of the job. But, for now, as I am left with none, your service would be welcome."

Byun bowed his head, "As you wish, young oracle."

"Come," Boreas said, "We must get through the rest of Gachichken quickly. We shall be safe once we reach Abyumo."

Vega stood, mentally saying *goodbye* to the old medicine man who had been her first keeper. Boreas lifted her into Breeze's saddle, climbing up in front of her. B leaped into Phoenix's saddle, and Byun climbed into Kimmi's. The four of them set out into the night, riding through Gachichken.

They rode through the next day, all of them exhausted when they finally made camp again. As they ate, readying themselves to catch up on sleep, Vega asked, "Why were we ambushed? Who would know or care enough about us to attack us?"

"I'm not sure," Boreas replied.

"It could be anyone in these lands," B inserted, "Gachichken has plenty of power-hungry leaders who would kill for the services of an oracle. How they would know about you, I'm not sure. We must tread carefully, and keep a watchful eye out."

"I shall take the first watch tonight," Byun said, "As Vega's new keeper, I feel it is my responsibility to keep her safe."

Boreas rolled his eyes. Vega wasn't sure she'd ever seen an elf do that before. It wasn't really in their nature. Though, she supposed, neither was teaming up with a dwarf. As they all lied down to get some sleep, her head was full of thoughts of how anyone would know who she was all the way out here, *Who were those men? Who sent them?*

As she drifted off, images of Fughar's slain body floated through her mind, *How did I not see that coming?*

They continued riding through Gachichken over the next week, trying to make it to the safety of Abyumo. As she sat on the back of Boreas' horse, a vision came to her. She saw herself, talking to B. They were standing in his throne room.

"The princess of the prophecy is your great-granddaughter," she told him.

"What?" he said, "Impossible."

"The rest of the world will know her as the only princess born from a great merged kingdom at the turn of the century. But you . . . You will know her as Celestia."

"No," B said, his face darkening, "You will not claim one of my descendants for your inane prophecy. She will be protected by so many layers of security, none of her 'warriors' will ever be able to reach her."

"But, B!" she said, "She must do this! She's the only one who can!"

"She 'must' do nothing!"

"If she doesn't, the world will be plunged into a hundred years of darkness!"

He glared at her, brown eyes narrowed, "The rest of the world is not my concern. Guards!"

"Don't do this, B!" she pleaded.

She watched as she was dragged from the throne room by King Boreas' guards.

When she snapped back to reality, she looked over at B. He was scratching his brown beard, seemingly unperturbed as he rode upon his black stallion. She never would have thought him capable of such a thing. But, more importantly, she knew she could never tell him about Celestia.

Her witch's glass began to vibrate in her pocket suddenly, and she lifted it, whispering, "Jezebelle?"

"Vega, another star just formed."

"Thank you," she said, "I think the pieces of this puzzle are starting to make sense."

"How are your travels going?" she asked.

"Not well," she replied, "Fughar is dead. We are in Gachichken, and we were ambushed in the night by soldiers. I'm not sure how much longer it will take to find a safe place."

"Fughar is dead?" Jezebelle asked, sounding surprised and forlorn, "I'm sorry, Vega. I hope you find a safe home soon. I'll call again when the next star forms. Hang in there. It's almost over."

"I'm not sure whether that's true, but . . . thanks."

She nodded, her pale face disappearing from the mirror's surface.

"You keep in contact with Jezebelle?" Boreas asked from in front of her.

"Yes," Vega replied, "She and I grew close in Gliken. Fughar was close with her as well . . . "

"I see," he said, "Did Gerard acquaint you?"

"Yes . . . ?" she answered questioningly.

Boreas nodded, continuing forward.

"Why?" she prodded.

"It's just that Gerard is loyal to Jurien."

"I know," she replied, "But he's a good man. He's only doing his duty to his king."

"Sometimes, duty isn't the right thing to do."

Vega was silent.

"He does love Jezebelle, though," he continued, "She's a smart woman. I always wondered what she sees in him."

"She *is* smart," she agreed, "And she loves him. She also supports the overthrowing of Jurien."

"Well, if what you told me is true, that will put her in an awkward position," Boreas said.

"Perhaps . . . " she said, thinking of poor Jezebelle, and wondering what Gerard would do when Jurien was overthrown.

They made it most of the way through Gachichken, riding all day, and finding secluded places to make camp by night. It gave Vega plenty of time to think about everything that had happened. She couldn't get the images of Fughar's body out of her head. She also continued to mull over her visions related to the prophecy. She had gathered that she was to say that a princess from a great merged kingdom, born at the turn of the century, would be the one to save the land from a terrible evil, with the help of a human warrior, a dwarven warrior, and an elven warrior. She wasn't sure what she was still missing, but she knew the remaining two visions would come.

The other question that continued to nag her was, *Who sent those soldiers to ambush us?* She wasn't sure she would ever get the answer to that. She thought perhaps she could induce a vision about it, but nothing came to her. She guessed it was because there was nothing in the future for her to see about it.

As soon as she'd thought it, they were all startled by another ambush. Several soldiers rode up on their horses, firing tiny arrows across them. Boreas began firing back, and B joined in. Byun lingered back a ways, waiting for the opportunity to use his axe.

Before they got close enough, B was hit with a dart. Then, before they could react, Byun was hit as well. As Boreas drew his sword, he was hit. When he slumped forward, Vega felt the stinging pain of something small and sharp sticking into the skin of her arm. Suddenly, everything went black.

Kiken

10

Vega awoke to the sensation of cold, hard stone beneath her. She sat up, looking around. She was in a dungeon cell, alone. It was all cold, gray stones on the walls and floor. There was one wall made of bars, and a barred window above her. It was tiny, and only a small bit of light poured in through the window and the hallway outside her cell. She felt the spot on her arm the dart had hit, and realized it had been a sleeping dart. There was a small poke mark where it had stuck her.

She slowly crept over to the barred wall, looking out into the dungeon. There were several cells along both sides, but none she could see into. She sighed, walking back to the back wall of her cell and sitting down. *Where am I?* she thought, *Where are Byun and the Boreases and Tabatha? What am I supposed to do?*

Suddenly, a guard appeared outside her cell, looking in at her. He waved down the hall and said, "She's awake!"

Vega stood slowly, leaning all the way back into the wall, frightened.

Another guard appeared beside the first, "Take her before King Adam."

The two guards opened her cell, entering. The first one grabbed her arm, pulling her along. The second took her other arm, and they led her down the dungeon corridor. As they passed the cells, she looked into each one, trying to find the others. But she didn't see them.

They took her up out of the dungeon, and to a palace throne room. A red-headed king sat upon the throne, perking up when they entered. "Vega, I believe," he said, "Am I right?"

The guards released her arms, pushing her forward. She looked up at the king, uncertain.

"I'm told you're an oracle," he looked her over, adding, "Well, not just any oracle. *The* Oracle."

Vega glared at him, "Is that why you sent your soldiers to ambush us?"

King Adam smirked, "Do you know how special you are?"

"Were they your soldiers the first time, too?" she demanded.

He sighed, rolling his eyes, "Yes, they were. Now, can we get to the more pressing issues?"

"No!" she shouted, "You killed Fughar!"

"What is she talking about?" he asked his guards, "Was someone in her company killed?"

They looked at each other nervously, one of them finally saying, "Yes. In the first wave, an old man was killed."

"Who killed him?" he demanded.

They looked at each other again, reluctantly saying, "It was Justin, sir."

King Adam paused, solemnly saying, "You know what to do."

They bowed, exiting the throne room.

"I'm very sorry about what happened to your travel companion," he said, turning his attention back to Vega, "Believe me, it will be dealt with."

"Where are the rest of them?" she demanded.

"They are all fine, I assure you," he said, "They will be released soon, so they can return to their homes and families. You will be allowed to say goodbye."

"*Allowed* to say *goodbye*?" she said, panicking, "What do you mean by that?"

"Vega, I'd like to talk to you, one on one. I'd like you to become Kiken's oracle."

"Kiken?"

"My kingdom, here in the land of Gachichken."

"I'm sorry, but . . . no. No way. I will not be the property of a single kingdom. I rule myself. I give my services to the world—the whole world."

"Maybe you didn't understand," Adam replied, a few of the guards he had posted around the room coming closer and pointing their spears at her, "You don't have a choice."

"Why are you doing this?" she asked, "How did you even know about me or find us?"

"I'm afraid that was my doing," a voice said. She turned to see a young woman with flowing brown hair, soulful brown eyes, and ample bosoms gliding into the room.

"Who are you?" Vega wondered.

"My name is Katrina," she said, "I am the current oracle of Kiken."

"You're an oracle?" she said, eyes wide. She had not expected to meet another oracle on her travels, and it excited her to know she was not the only one.

The woman nodded, "I saw you coming. I knew where you would be, and when."

"How did I not see you?" she asked in disbelief.

Katrina smirked, "Because I blocked you."

"What? How?" Vega couldn't believe what she was hearing.

"Oracles can block other oracles from seeing things they don't want them to see."

She gawked at her, still trying to process the things she never knew. She wondered what else she could do that she didn't yet know how to. After a long pause, she finally said, "Why are you doing this? Why sabotage one of your own?"

"I'm ready to retire," Katrina said, "I've earned it after all these years. My head hurts from so many visions. I saw you, and I knew you would make the perfect replacement. Plus, I don't like you. I think you're arrogant to call yourself *The* Oracle, when there are so many of us out there."

"I don't call myself *The* Oracle!" Vega yelled, "Other people call me that! I never wanted any of this! I just wanted to be a normal kid!"

"Oracles don't have that luxury," King Adam interjected, "Now, enough of this. You'll return to the dungeon until you can accept that you are Kiken's new oracle. If you can't accept it by tomorrow, you'll lose your chance to say goodbye to your companions before they're released. Take her away."

"No!" Vega yelled, trying to fight the guards as two of them began dragging her back to the dungeon. As a mere child, she didn't have the strength to overcome two brawny men. Nevertheless, she kicked and flailed the whole way back to her cell.

Once the guards had thrown her inside, she began to cry hopelessly.

"Vega?" a voice asked.

She gasped, looking around, "Hello?"

"Vega, is that you?" the voice said.

"Yes, who are you?" she asked, trying to figure out where it was coming from, and why it sounded familiar.

"It's me, Byun," he answered.

"Byun!" she cried, happy to know he was alive as she'd been told, "Where are you?"

"I'm in the cell to the left of yours."

"Are you alright?" she asked.

"I'm fine," he replied, "You?"

"I'm not hurt, if that's what you mean. But, I just spoke with the king, and he's forcing me to become the kingdom oracle! He plans to release the rest of you tomorrow, and keep me here."

"I figured as much," he said.

"Where are the others?" she asked.

"Boreas and Boreas are in cells further down the hall," Byun said, "And your pixie friend is in a jar on the guards' desk."

"What about the horses?"

He sighed, "I'm not sure. I assume they're in the royal stables, but I don't know."

Vega leaned against the wall between their cells, unsure what to say or do next.

Byun was silent as she sat, pondering.

Finally, she said, "They have an oracle who's retiring. She saw us. She saw me. That's how they knew where to find us. She blocked me. That's why I didn't see it coming. That's why I didn't see that Fughar was going to die . . . "

"I'm sorry," Byun said softly, "It's not your fault, Vega. You had no way of knowing."

She began to sob quietly, letting a few tears roll down.

After a long pause, he said, "They won't get away with this. As your new keeper, and in honor of Fughar, I vow that you will not become *any* kingdom's oracle. We're getting out of here."

"H-how?" she asked, trying to stop her tears.

"Don't worry about it," he replied, "I'll take care of it."

Vega was left to wonder what Byun meant, and how he intended to "take care of it." She curled up against the cold, hard stone of her cell to try and get some sleep.

Vega awoke to distant yells echoing through the dungeon. She sat up, trying to make out the sound. She realized it was getting closer. She hopped up, backing toward her cell wall. Suddenly, a tin can rolled into the bars of her cage wall. The top of it was sparking with flame. When it hit a bar, it exploded. Vega shielded her eyes as dust and debris blew around her cell. When she looked up, and the smoke cleared, there was Byun, garbed in a guard's uniform.

"Vega, let's go," he said, "Come on!" He grabbed her hand, and the two of them ran out into the corridor.

"Where are the others?" she asked.

As soon as she'd said it, the Boreases came charging through in their guard uniforms.

"We don't have much time!" B shouted.

"Let's get her out of here!" Boreas added.

"Wait, where's Tabatha?" Vega asked, looking around, "I won't leave without her!"

"I'll get her!" Boreas yelled, turning around, "Just go!"

"Come on!" B shouted.

B and Byun pulled Vega along—running up the stairs, and out of the dungeon. There were other prisoners running all around them, and the guards were unable to catch everyone in the chaos. They ran straight to the stables, and luckily, Breeze, Phoenix, and Kimmi were there.

The two men readied the three horses quickly, preparing to set out. Vega looked around worriedly, hoping Boreas and Tabatha would make it. It didn't take long before the horses were ready, and B leaped upon Phoenix's back, ready to lead the way. Byun lifted Vega into Kimmi's saddle, climbing up in front of her.

"Wait!" Vega cried, "We can't leave them behind!"

"They'll catch up!" Byun shouted, "We can't waste time. They're after *you*!"

With that, they rode out of the stable, trampling any guards that got in their way. B led the way into the nearby forest, trying to make cover before they realized where she was. They rode hard, leaving Kiken far behind them.

They continued through the night, not daring to stop, even to make camp. They were exhausted the next day, but they kept going. They knew they wouldn't be safe until they reached Abyumo. Vega continued to worry about Boreas and her little pixie friend. They hadn't caught up with them, and she hoped they had made it out okay.

Just then, she had a vision. Katrina was standing before King Adam.

"How could you let them get away?" he shouted, "You're telling me you didn't see them escaping?"

Katrina was silent, staring at the king. When she looked into the distance, it appeared to Vega that she was looking directly at her. Suddenly, she winked, and Vega realized she was sharing this vision with her. She had let them escape!

As the vision faded, they heard the sound of hooves hitting the earth behind them. When they looked back, they saw Breeze coming through the trees with Boreas on his back. They all smiled, happy to see they'd made it out.

"Ride!" Boreas shouted, "They're coming after us!"

They began riding hard again, their poor, overworked horses exhaustedly running.

"We're almost to Abyumo!" Boreas shouted.

"We'll never make it!" B said.

They all looked back to see the guards of Kiken catching up to them. Their horses couldn't run any faster, all their energy drained from the last couple of days without rest. As they rode, they realized B was right: they weren't going to make it.

Suddenly, a blinding light shone ahead of them. As they looked, it got brighter, and they had to shield their eyes. It shone past them, and when they looked back, they saw the guards were blasted back into the forest.

When it died down, they saw that a wizard had conjured it. He was an ancient man with a long, thin, gray beard and golden eyes. He looked each of them over, piercing them with his stare. "What brings you to the realm of the wizards?" he asked, lowering his staff.

"We come seeking sanctuary," Boreas said.

"Our magic is not for outsiders to use whenever they decide," he retorted.

Vega had been sitting behind Byun, staring at the wizard in awe. Now, this was the kind of keeper she needed! Upon hearing his reply, she snapped out of it, saying, "I am an oracle, looking for a place to call home."

"Not just an oracle," Byun added, "*The* Oracle."

B perked up, "She was chosen by the Tree of Knowledge itself in the elven forest."

The wizard's eyes widened. After a pause, he said, "Come with me."

They all followed the old man into Abyumo. He led them to a nearby pond, casting a spell over it, "*Balgadeer.*"

A group of old wizards appeared upon the water's surface.

"Fellow councilmen," he began, "I have called this meeting to determine whether we shall allow the relocation of a new resident."

A few of them began whispering to each other. Finally, one of them asked, "Is he or she there with you, Thrindil?"

Thrindil nodded. He turned, beckoning for Vega to come closer. She climbed off the back of Byun's horse, walking over while they watched.

"Tell them your name," he said.

She stepped to the edge of the pond, staring at all the old, weathered faces in it, "My name is Vega."

"And, what powers do you possess, Vega?" they asked.

"She is an oracle," Thrindil replied for her.

"Oracle?" they questioned, "That is most unusual."

"Yes, but technically they do possess abilities that could be deemed magical," Thrindil said.

They all chattered amongst themselves for a few minutes, trying to determine whether they should let her stay.

As they were doing so, Vega was struck with another vision. She was back in Kataran. Cassie was there, an old woman. She was standing before the new Council of Elders. "The Great Prophecy states that the human warrior is born in the village of Chance. Chance is spelled with a capital C. Therefore, it is a name. Now, as our esteemed Council of Elders, I trust you all know what our village of Kataran's name means."

They looked at each other, unsure.

Cassie smiled, "It means, 'chance.' Therefore, the prophecy is referring to *our* village."

There were wide eyes and shocked whispers as they excitedly realized what she was saying.

"He is said to be the one who can solve the unsolvable riddle," she continued.

After some more whispering, one of them asked, "What's the 'unsolvable riddle,' then?"

"I hoped you would ask," she said, pulling a scroll from the folds of her dress, "It was entrusted to me by a dwarven messenger, sent to us from The Oracle herself. It details the entire prophecy, including the riddle."

There were several gasps, and more whispers, as they stared in amazement at the scroll in her hand.

"The riddle is to be presented to any young man who wishes to attempt it. The one who solves it will become the warrior of the prophecy. It says, 'Born from ash, to ash return, but not all of us will burn.'"

They looked at each other in confusion, none of them able to figure it out.

As the vision faded, Vega blinked her eyes clear, seeing that the wizard council had vanished from the water's surface. "What happened?" she asked, "Did they decide to let me stay?"

Thrindil

11

"You had another vision, didn't you?" Jezebelle asked from the witch's glass.

"Yes," Vega replied, "Another star formed?"

The silver-haired elf nodded.

"Then, there is only one star left?" Vega asked.

"And one vision left to complete your prophecy," Jezebelle confirmed.

"After I have the last one, I shall tell you the prophecy. I'll trust you to give it to your people."

The elf-witch nodded, "I will." After a pause, she asked, "What about you? Have you found a safe place to call home?"

"Sort of," she replied.

"Sort of?"

"Well, I have found refuge in the realm of the wizards in Abyumo. But, I must still find an actual home. They've granted me residency, but I don't have a place to live yet. We're staying in one of the wizard councilman's homes until I find something. Once my prophecy is complete, I shall send

Boreas back home. He has helped get me safely here, and even rescued my pixie friend, Tabatha. He has done his part. B has done the same, and he shall return to Duwazo when this is over. As for our dwarven companion, he will be sent with the important mission of delivering the prophecy to the dwarves, and to the village of Kataran in Katangalo."

"Then, who will stay with you?" she asked.

"I must find a new keeper," she said, "Hopefully, before the last vision."

"You plan to look for one among the wizards?"

Vega nodded, "I think a wizard would be the perfect keeper. They would be powerful enough to protect me better than any others."

Jezebelle nodded, "Good luck, Vega." With that, her image faded from view.

Vega looked around the room she had been provided in Thrindil's house. It was warm and cozy, and reminded her of a more luxurious version of her room back home. Tabatha flitted about, stretching her wings. After being cooped up in a jar, she was happy to be free to fly around.

Byun and the Boreases each had their own room as well. Thrindil was kind enough to open his home to them, albeit temporarily. Vega knew she was close to the end of her prophecy, and she needed to find a home and a keeper soon, or she wouldn't be able to send her companions back. She planned to start her search the following day. She wasn't sure how difficult it would be to find either one. As she curled up into bed, she watched the glowing, ivory sparks from her pixie friend trailing back and forth. Her mind was filled with what she needed to do, and how she could do it. Her final thought as she fell asleep was, *Lord, help me find someone wise, compassionate, brave, and powerful to be my keeper . . .*

When Vega awoke, she got dressed hurriedly, ready to begin her search. Tabatha tagged along as she walked out into the main room of the house. Thrindil was drinking a cup of coffee and reading a book. He looked up when he saw her, "Good morning, Vega. Sleep well?"

She nodded, "Hey, Thrindil? I'm in the market for a keeper. My first was a frail old medicine man. He was killed on our travels. Now, Byun has offered to take his place, but I only agreed to it temporarily. You see, I realized I need someone more powerful to protect me. There are many out there who would use my powers to their own ends. I think I need a wizard."

He looked at her steadily, contemplating, "If you can find one willing, then perhaps that would be your best bet. But, the search will not be easy."

"Well, what about you?" she asked, "Your magic helped us get across the border. You are very powerful, indeed. And, you seem to have plenty of space here, all to yourself."

"Me?" he said, "Oh, no. I'm sorry, Vega, but I am our head councilman. It's a full-time job. I just can't spare the time to become your keeper. I live alone for a reason. I like my space and my privacy. You'll be hard-pressed to find someone around here who doesn't."

She looked down, discouraged.

"You're a brilliant young lady," Thrindil added, "But, being an oracle's keeper requires a lot. I'm not sure you understand what you're asking. They must dedicate their whole life to you. They must always care for you, provide for you, facilitate your exchanges, and protect you at all costs. It's a big job."

"Then, I am selfish to ask it of anyone. Yet, if I do not find someone powerful who is willing to do it, then I will be a child alone in the world. No one will be able to shield me from those who would use me. It's an impossible situation to be in."

"Well, you've already found two keepers willing to do the job," he said, "And, one of them got you here safely, helping you escape from a king who wanted to use you. Though he is not as powerful as a wizard, he is brave and true."

Vega nodded.

"You are not alone," Thrindil said.

She knew he was right, and that Byun was a good man, and one willing to do the job. But, she also knew that he wouldn't be able to protect her from everything. He barely got her away from King Adam's army. She sighed, feeling hopeless.

She went for a walk around the hills where Thrindil lived. The beautiful, ancient flowers whispered in the wind. The blades of grass tickled her legs beneath her brown peasant's dress. She lied down, looking up at the clouds. Tabatha flitted about the hillside happily, trailing her ivory pixie dust behind her.

Just then, she had a vision. She saw a silver-haired witch with violet eyes and flowing, glittery robes. Despite her age, she was beautiful. She was wandering along the hills where Vega lay, smiling to herself. Her smile was radiant.

A wizard approached from the other side of the hill. He had a chest-length beard and navy blue robes. "Theodora," he said, his blue eyes twinkling, "I'm so glad you came."

"Rigel," she replied, rushing into his arms, "Of course I did. I love you."

They kissed, and he said, "Let us leave this place, my darling. I shall build a life for us in the northern reaches of Abyumo."

Theodora nodded, "I'm with you. Let's go."

Rigel smiled, and they kissed again. He scooped her into his arms, and the two of them laughed as they ran through the hills, toward the north.

As Vega came back to the present, she wondered what that vision could mean, *I saw something good happening for once? Why? What purpose could it serve? Who were those people? Was this somehow related to the prophecy?*

She needed answers, but she wasn't sure she could get them. She headed back to Thrindil's house, hoping somehow he might have answers.

"Vega, I was wondering where you wandered off to," Byun said as she entered, "I was worried."

"Have we completed our mission, yet?" B asked, sounding somewhat annoyed.

"Not yet," she said, "But, I believe your part in this is over. You are free to go home whenever you're ready."

"We are?" Boreas asked, "How do you know? What purpose did we even serve?"

"Human Boreas, yes," Vega clarified, "But not you and Byun. Not yet. I'll let you know when I have the answers. It will be soon. I'm just not sure exactly when."

Boreas looked down solemnly, and she could tell that he wanted to return home to his family and his people.

B looked confused, "Why me? Why am I free to go and not them? What purpose did I serve?"

"We wouldn't have made it here without you," she replied, "These two alone wouldn't have been enough. As for why you specifically, you sparked certain visions in me . . . visions pertaining to the prophecy. I'm not sure why. Perhaps you have a bit of magic in you. Anyway, I know your part in this is over, because I had a vision of you returning home to Duwazo."

"You saw my kingdom?" he asked.

Vega nodded, "And, I saw your family. They are waiting for you. They have something to tell you."

His brown eyes grew wide, "You had a vision about *me*?"

"Thank you for your service," she said, "You are closer to your home now. Go, and discover for yourself what your family has in store for you."

B nodded excitedly, "Thank you, Vega!"

As he rushed to gather his things and leave, she muttered, "Don't thank me yet."

Boreas eyed her suspiciously, his dark eyes narrowed, "What did you see?"

She turned to look at the tall, dark elf, "His son is engaged. I'm not sure whether that will be happy news for him or not. She's . . . not from around here."

He continued to stare at her, still suspicious, "His son is five years old."

She looked at him in surprise, "I didn't realize how far in the future my vision was."

He kept his eyes fixed on her, "That doesn't seem like a very good reason, anyway."

She shifted uncomfortably, not wanting to tell him the truth.

"Is that really your *only* reason?" he probed.

Vega sighed, "I can't tell him the prophecy. If I do, he'll jeopardize its success. So, there is no reason for him to stay."

Boreas gasped, "You have foreseen this?"

She nodded, "Yes. I wouldn't have believed he would do something like that. But now that I know, I cannot trust him with this." She paused, "He's not a bad man. There's just an aspect of this prophecy that he won't be able to handle. I hope this doesn't change your opinion of him. And, I hope you will respect my wishes and not say anything."

He nodded, his black hair falling over his shoulders.

When B returned, his saddlebags packed, he said his goodbyes, hugging each of them, "It's been an honor, Vega, Byun." He lingered on Boreas, "I'll miss you, my brother. 'Til we meet again."

The dark elf nodded, hugging his friend, "I shall miss you as well . . . my brother."

B headed out, getting Phoenix from the stable and setting out for Duwazo.

When Vega was once again alone with Thrindil, she asked, "Do you know a witch named Theodora?"

He looked up at her, surprised, "How do you know Theodora?"

"Umm . . . I don't," she said, "I had a vision about her."

"Really?" he asked, "What was this vision?"

Vega paused, unsure how much she should say, "I think it would be best if I spoke with her directly. Do you think you could arrange a meeting?"

Thrindil paused, eyeing her suspiciously, "Very well. I can arrange for her and Thaandor to be here tomorrow."

"Thaandor?" she asked.

"Yes," he said, "Thaandor is her fiancé."

Vega tried to hide her reaction from Thrindil. *So, that's why I had this vision,* she thought, *She's going to leave her fiancé for another man.*

"Is everything alright, Vega?" Thrindil asked.

"Yes, I'm fine," she replied, "Just thinking about what I'm going to say to her."

He nodded, going back to his book.

"Vega, I'd like you to meet Theodora," Thrindil said, gesturing grandly as the beautiful witch from her vision entered his house, "Theodora, this is Vega. She's an oracle."

"An oracle?" she asked, "How exciting!"

A wizard in light blue robes walked in behind her. He had a beard that went to his knees, and brown eyes. He was very different from the man in her vision.

"And, this is Thaandor," Thrindil continued, "Theodora's fiancé."

"Pleasure to meet you," Thaandor said, giving her a nod.

Vega nodded back, feeling a knot in her gut. She wasn't sure whether she should tell him what was going to happen.

"Please, let us all sit down to tea," Thrindil said, "I've already laid everything out."

"Oh, thank you, Thrindil," Theodora said, "This looks lovely."

The four of them entered the sitting room, where Thrindil had the table set with tea and cookies. They began eating and drinking and engaging in polite conversation. It seemed it had been a while since they'd seen each other, as they were catching up. It gave Vega a minute to try to clear her head.

"Vega here had a vision about you she'd like to share," Thrindil said, turning to her, "Vega?"

She took a long sip of tea, gulping before she said, "Umm . . . it's really something that should be discussed in private."

"Nonsense," he said, "We're all friends here. There's nothing I don't know about these two."

"I bet you don't know this," she mumbled.

"What's that?" he asked.

"Nothing," she replied, "It's more like a . . . girl thing. I don't feel comfortable talking about it with you two in the room."

"Very well," Thaandor said, "Come on, Thrindil. I can take a hint."

The two wizards headed outside, leaving Vega alone with Theodora.

"What is it you wanted to tell me?" she asked.

"You two seem like a lovely couple," she said, evading the question.

Theodora cleared her throat, looking uncomfortable, "Yes. We are."

"Do you love him?" she asked.

She looked away, unanswering.

After a pause, Vega said, "If you don't love him, why are you with him?"

Theodora sighed, "There are things your young mind wouldn't understand."

"Try me," she replied, looking at her steadily.

She sized her up before finally saying, "Very well. I like Thaandor a lot. Our families are very close. He loves me. We just make sense. When he asked me to marry him, I couldn't think of a good reason to say no."

"But you want to," she said. It wasn't a question.

She sighed again, "Yes. I want to say no. I don't want to marry Thaandor. I don't love him. At least, not the way he loves me."

"Then why don't you tell him that?" she asked, "That seems like a pretty good reason to me."

Theodora looked away, "I know how he feels about me. I don't want to break his heart. I just feel terrible. No one else would understand. My family, my friends . . . they all want me to marry him. I feel like I can't escape."

"Is that why you plan to run away with Rigel?"

Her violet eyes widened, "How do you know about Rigel?"

She looked at her steadily, not saying anything.

"You really are an oracle," she said.

"Not just an oracle," Vega replied, "*The* Oracle."

The Prophecy

12

"**D**id you and Theodora have a good chat?" Thrindil asked as he and Thaandor returned to the sitting room.

"Yes, I think I said everything I needed to say," Vega said, eyeing Theodora meaningfully.

She gulped, quickly recovering her facade, "Seeing into the future is such a fascinating talent, don't you agree, Thaandor?"

He looked at her questioningly, "Indeed. It's a gift I'm not sure I'd want to possess."

"Thaandor," she reprimanded.

"It's alright," Vega said, "It's not a gift I ever wanted, either. Truth be told, it's more of a burden."

Thaandor smiled, "I can see how it would be, especially for one so young."

"Many people covet my skills," she said, "I must always have a keeper to keep them at bay."

"I'm sure finding one is no easy feat, either," he replied.

She chuckled, "No, it isn't."

"Well, thank you for having us, Thrindil," Theodora said, "But, I think it's time Thaandor and I leave."

"Yes," Thaandor agreed, "It was a pleasure meeting you, Vega."

She shook his hand, unsure what she could say to this kind, old wizard whose heart would soon be broken. Thrindil walked them out, saying his goodbyes. She sat there pondering, wishing she could have done more.

The next day, Vega resolved to search for a place to live. Byun, Boreas, and even Tabatha accompanied her as they rode through the realm of the wizards. They encountered many different homes, all belonging to a witch or wizard.

"Are there no unoccupied homes around here?" Vega asked.

"I suppose each one was constructed by the witch or wizard who occupies it," Byun said.

Boreas sighed, "When someone is granted residency, they must find a home on their own. By 'find,' I can only assume they mean magically construct."

Vega groaned hopelessly, "How am I supposed to 'magically construct' a house when I cannot wield magic?" After a pause, it hit her. She stopped in her tracks, grinning from ear to ear.

Boreas and Byun looked at her curiously.

"What?" Byun asked.

"I need to find the proper instruction," she said, "Let's head back. I need to talk to Thrindil."

They rode back to his house, the two men continuing to stare at her in confusion.

Once they'd put Kimmi and Breeze back in the stable, they entered the house, going straight to Thrindil.

"How do you construct a house with magic?" she asked.

He, too, stared at her questioningly, "Why do you ask, young oracle? I see not how it would benefit you."

"It will make sense in due time," she replied, "Just please, can you teach me?"

He sighed, "I'm afraid I have council matters I must attend to, but . . . perhaps Thaandor would be willing to teach you. He's still figuring out where his talents can be of the most use, so he's not obligated to be anywhere. I shall give him a call."

"Thank you," Vega said.

It didn't take long for Thaandor to arrive, ready to teach her. He led her to an empty plain near the border to the realm of the dragon riders.

"The key to any spell is to tune in to your current of magic, allowing it to flow through you. It's most difficult your first time. To construct a house, you must concentrate hard, and visualize the structure you wish to create. It's a very advanced spell. I wouldn't advise it your first time. It may not come out right."

"Unfortunately, I don't really have the luxury of a trial spell," she said.

"Very well," Thaandor said, "The incantation is '*Stucco*.' Good luck."

"Thank you, Thaandor," she said, "And, thank you for not asking questions."

He nodded, giving her a smile, "I've learned that in life, it's better not to ask. If you're meant to know something, you'll learn it."

Vega tuned in to the current of power the nymphs had gifted her. *Please work,* she thought. She pictured the way she wanted her home to look, visualizing it clearly in her mind. When she felt ready, she held up her hands, saying, "*Stucco*."

She opened her eyes to see the colorful rainbow of the nymphs' magic streaming from her fingertips. As her house began to take shape, Thaandor raised his staff, aiding her. It formed into an elliptical, ivory structure, with smooth walls and a pair of large doors on the front.

"Is this what you envisioned?" Thaandor asked.

Vega smiled, "Yes, it is. Care for a tour?"

"Why not?" he said.

She led him inside, where it had a cozy front room with insulated walls and cushioned floors. Through a door on the back wall, it led into the main part of the house. There was a kitchen/dining area, and a short corridor with four doors. One leading to the bathroom, one to a closet, one to a guest bedroom, and one to Vega's new bedroom. With the exception of the front room, all the rooms were furnished. Her room had a soft, luxurious bed, a long end table with drawers, and a sleek wardrobe. It even had a tiny replica of her bed upon a shelf in the corner. It was for Tabatha to sleep on, right beside the window.

"Impressive," Thaandor said, "I've never seen anything like it."

"Thank you," she replied, "And thank you for helping me create it. I couldn't have done it without you."

"If I may ask, why is the front room unfurnished?"

Vega smiled, "It is the perfect place for meetings with those who come seeking my visions. I can sit comfortably meditating on the floor, and view the future. It is apart from the rest of my home, so others will never see this part. I can keep it to myself. It will be vision-free. It will be my private sanctuary . . . "

"I see," he said, nodding, "You are a brilliant young lady, indeed."

"As for the magic," she said, "you know I can't wield it, right?"

He nodded.

"I received a gift from the nymphs in the forest of the elves. They granted me enough of their magic to perform one spell." She gestured around her, "This was it."

Thaandor smiled, "You chose well."

She paused. After a long minute, she said, "I don't know if you know this, but . . . I'm looking for a keeper. Byun—my dwarven companion—is filling in temporarily, but he's not powerful enough to protect me long-term. Thrindil is busy with the wizard council." She paused again, "I was wondering if . . . maybe . . . you would want the job."

"Me?" he said, surprised, "I . . . umm . . . I'm flattered, Vega. But, I'm afraid I can't accept. I'm getting married soon, and I need to find a job that pays well. I also couldn't devote as much time as you would require, as I'd like to spend a fair amount of time with my wife."

She nodded, unsure whether she should tell him what she'd seen. Just then, a vision came to her. She was standing on a ferry near the kingdom of Khanjgi. As she looked around, she saw Princess Celestia, Bridgot, Kgansten, and Aurano. She also saw a dark-skinned woman with green eyes she didn't recognize. As she watched, a couple of vekkens began to attack them. The massive creatures were terrifying to behold. They slithered through the sky like two serpents circling their prey. Just then, a green dragon flew out from the trees, attacking one of them.

The warriors on the ferry began battling the second, and Bridgot jumped in front of Celestia to protect her, stabbing the vekken. It shrieked, clutching him in its claw as it fell into the water. The rest of them yelled after him, but it was too late, and Bridgot was dragged to the depths of the river.

The vision shifted, and she was standing inside the dark castle of Khanjgi, where Nazirdok was performing his ritual. Celestia, Kgansten, and Aurano fought their hardest, trying to stop him, but they couldn't. Celestia was too heart-broken to fight after Bridgot's death. Nazirdok completed his ritual, the wave of dark power that exploded around him instantly dissolving the three of them.

"No!" Vega yelled, wondering how she could change that.

It shifted again, and she saw herself sitting in her front room. She was older, and she was wearing a turquoise top with sheer arms and turquoise pants with sheer legs, her stomach visible between the two. Bridgot, Kgansten, and Aurano stood before her.

"You three are the warriors I prophesied about," she said to them, "You all have a part to play before this quest is over."

"What do you mean?" Bridgot asked.

"Trust Celestia. She will not lead you astray. Stay true to each other and remain strong. Only together can you succeed."

"No problem there," Kgansten said, "The three of us are the strongest of warriors."

She frowned, looking at them sadly, "There is something else I must tell you. One of you will die to save the princess before this quest is over. And, it must happen if you are to succeed."

"What?" they said in unison.

"I'm sorry," she replied, "But, that's the way it has to be. There's no other way. Go now. You're running out of time."

As it shifted again, she saw flashes of Celestia diving into the water . . . pulling Bridgot back onto the ferry . . . and a thought echoing through her mind, only it was Celestia's voice, *He's not going to die saving me. I don't care what The Oracle said* . . .

So that's the key! Vega thought, *If I tell them that, he'll live!*

The vision shifted again, back to the castle in Khanjgi. They were all battling Nazirdok, Bridgot included. Suddenly, Celestia broke free of his spell, blue powers radiating around her, and knocking Nazirdok back.

She's a witch? Vega thought, *Of course! That's why she can defeat him!*

Celestia made her way to the table full of ritual objects in the center of the room. As Nazirdok reached his feet, he cast a curse to stop her, and Aurano jumped in front of her. It hit him instead, and as Celestia flipped the table, Vega could see that he was dead.

Nazirdok was defeated, but it would cost Aurano his life. Then, she realized what this vision meant. If she didn't say anything to them, Bridgot would die. If he died, they would fail to fulfill the prophecy. If she said something, Aurano would die instead. But, his death would mean their success, and the saving of the world.

As she was contemplating what she should do, the vision shifted yet again. She was in the realm of the dragon riders. She stood in a glistening emerald palace before a queen with auburn hair and golden armor. A massive amber dragon was asleep beside her.

"Kirstiana," Thaandor said to her, "You know why we have come."

Celestia, Bridgot, Kgansten, and Aurano stood beside him.

"Yes," Kirstiana said, "I have appointed you a dragon rider warrior, as per the prophecy. His name is Emil. He and his dragon, Jade, are ready to set out."

"Excellent," he replied, "So are they."

It shifted again, and they were back on the ferry in Khanjgi. Jade was getting ripped apart by the two vekkens as Emil watched helplessly. Jade was a deep blue-green colored dragon, and Emil was a pale-skinned elf with silver hair and jade eyes. When they made it to the other side, Jade was tossed into the trees, and Emil ran after her. Once they'd killed them, they pursued the rest of them, ripping through Bridgot and Kgansten as Celestia got her powers.

She and Aurano fought them off, but by the time they'd killed them, they were too weak to continue into Khanjgi. They were badly injured, and in no shape to attempt to fight a dark wizard. They lied on the hillside, bleeding into the earth as Nazirdok completed his ritual, his darkness spreading over the land.

She remembered the dark-skinned human dragon rider woman she had seen from her previous vision of the ferry, and realized she was the one destined to accompany them on their quest. *So, I can't mention the dragon riders, either,* she thought, *If I do, they'll appoint Emil, and the quest will fail.*

It shifted again, and she was back in Khanjgi's castle. They were battling Nazirdok, but this time, the woman was with them. As soon as Nazirdok realized she was a dragon rider, he cast a wave of dark magic over them, killing them all.

"No!" she screamed again. The visions were becoming too much for her, as she'd never had this many in a row before, and her head was exploding with pain, but it shifted again.

She saw her older self in her front room again. The dragon rider woman was there.

"Nastazya," she said, "I'm pleased to see you came to visit me before you set out tomorrow."

"Of course," Nastazya replied, "I must know what I'm up against before we leave."

"You must all get to Khanjgi before the stars align in a fortnight, and stop the dark wizard, Nazirdok from conducting his ritual. If you fail, the world will be plunged into darkness for a hundred years. If you succeed, the world will know peace for as long."

She nodded, her tight, twisted bun moving with her head.

"There is something else I must tell you as well. This fight is not meant for you. Though you can wield magic, you must not do anything rash or foolish. He's too strong. You need to know the extent of what you can do, and of what *he* can do. He has access to other sources of energy and power. You'll jeopardize the entire quest if you try to fight him."

Finally, she came back to reality, collapsing to the floor as Thaandor tried to catch her.

Vega awoke in Thrindil's living room with Thrindil, Thaandor, Boreas, and Byun sitting around her. The witch's glass in her pocket was buzzing. It matched the ringing in her ears and the throbbing in her head.

"Are you alright?" Thaandor asked.

She nodded, sitting up slowly, "I had the final vision of this prophecy."

As they stared, she pulled out her witch's glass, watching Jezebelle's face appear before her.

"Vega? Did you have the final vision?"

"Yes," she replied, "I'm ready to share it now."

"All seven stars have formed," Jezebelle said.

Vega nodded, "It is finished."

As they all continued to stare at her, she said, "A princess from a great merged kingdom, born at the turn of the century, will be the one to save the land from a terrible evil, with the help of a great warrior, solver of the unsolvable riddle, born in the village of Chance. In order to ensure success, a warrior from each of the races of elf and dwarf must also aid our victors."

There was a long pause as everyone took in what she'd said.

"I'll let our people know of this," Jezebelle said finally, breaking the silence, "I will do my best to ensure we provide an elven warrior to aid the cause."

"Thank you," Vega said, "Don't be a stranger."

With that, Jezebelle's face faded from view.

When they continued to sit in silence, Vega said, "Boreas, I must assign you the task of bearing this prophecy to your people. Though Jezebelle will try to spread the word, I know the elves will take more convincing. The people will listen to you. That is why you were the one to accompany me on this quest."

Boreas nodded solemnly.

"Byun," she said, turning to him, "As soon as I am able to find a new keeper, I'm entrusting you with the task of bringing the prophecy to your people, the dwarves."

"Of course," Byun said, bowing his head.

"You will also be entrusted with a second task," she continued, "You must take the prophecy, along with the unsolvable riddle, to the village of Kataran in Katangalo. Give it to a girl named Cassie. Trust no one else. Tell her it's from me. Tell her to look up what the name 'Kataran' means. Tell her to present it to the Council of Elders when her first grandchild is born."

Byun nodded, "It shall be done."

"So, I am free to set out?" Boreas asked.

Vega nodded, "Yes. You may head back to the land of the elves. Your people need you now."

He nodded in agreement, acknowledging his duty.

"Your *family* needs you now," she added.

He looked down, his pointed ears twitching with sadness.

She took his hand, "Tell Kamine hello for me when you see her."

"I will," he replied.

As their hands touched, she was struck with yet another vision. She was standing in the elven kingdom of Garellis. Thaddeus and Gerard were arguing.

"Jurien is no longer our king," Thaddeus said, "He must pay for his crimes against our people."

As she watched, she realized Jurien was there, tied up on the ground before them. A large crowd was assembled, watching with anticipation, curiosity, or concern.

"We're not going to kill him," Gerard said.

"I know you're loyal to him," Thaddeus replied, "I don't want to have to kill you, too."

"I *was* loyal to him. As you said, he is no longer our king. I remain loyal to whoever sits upon that throne. But, I do not believe in killing our own. Violence is never the solution."

"The only way to ensure he doesn't come back to destroy us is to ensure he doesn't come back," he retorted.

Several of the warriors who'd stormed the palace cheered in agreement.

"We can't do that," Gerard said, "We're not killers."

"Maybe *you* are not a killer," Thaddeus replied, "But, *we* are warriors. Our job is to kill."

"Our job is to protect our people," he said.

"Yes," he agreed, "And the only way to ensure their safety is to kill him . . . and anyone who gets in our way."

Gerard looked up, meeting his eyes, "What are you saying?"

"Gentlemen," Thaddeus said to his men, "Tie him up."

The other warriors surrounded Gerard, starting to tie him up like Jurien.

"No! Stop!" Jezebelle shouted, running into the clearing.

"Jezebelle," Gerard said, staring at her.

"Yes?" Thaddeus asked, "What input does a librarian bring?"

Jezebelle hurried to Gerard's side, untying him and making sure he was alright. She stood tall, speaking to the crowd, "Is this the grace and prudence of the elven race? We are not barbarians. We are civilized. We can determine an appropriate punishment besides death. We also should be thinking more about who will replace him than about what torment he should face. Do we not leave punishments up to our monarchs? Who put you in charge? Are you trying to become the new king, Thaddeus?"

There were several shouts of agreement, as people began to realize it wasn't right for him to decide what they should do with Jurien.

He glared at Jezebelle, "Very well. I say we call a vote, then. Do I hear any nominations for our new king?"

"I nominate Thaddeus!" one of the warriors shouted.

"I nominate Gerard!" someone in the crowd shouted.

"I nominate Jezebelle!" someone else shouted.

"I nominate Boreas," Thaddeus said smugly.

Jezebelle smiled, "I second that."

Thaddeus looked at her in surprise.

"All in favor of appointing Boreas the new king," Gerard said, raising his hand.

Almost everyone in the crowd and amongst the warriors raised their hands.

"Then, it's settled," Jezebelle said, "Boreas is the new king of Garellis. And as such, it is *his* decision what we do with Jurien."

"Since he's not here, and I'm his right-hand man," Thaddeus said, "I say we kill him."

"Who says I'm not here?" Boreas said, riding up on Breeze's back.

Everyone looked up in surprise.

"Nominated and appointed king without anyone telling *me*?" he looked around, "How does that happen?"

"Boreas," Thaddeus said, "I'm glad you're back."

"What if I said no? That would put everyone in an awkward situation, wouldn't it?"

"We would just appoint someone else," Gerard said, "It is up to you whether you accept the role."

Thaddeus hurried over to Boreas' horse, "Sir, we must make an example of Jurien."

"And you, Thaddeus," he said, "I'm disappointed in you. You are supposed to be brave, honorable, and wise. Yet, before me, I see someone cowardly, shameful, and foolish."

"Sir?" he said, shocked.

"You think dragging the king from his castle and killing him in front of the crowd is the right thing to do? You want to make an example of him. But, is that the kind of example you want to set for our people?"

"But, he could build an army, come back later, and attack us," he replied.

"Build an army? Do you hear yourself? He is weak; he is defeated. There is no army that would heed his call. And, if he does manage to amass one, that is what our kingdom's defenses are for. The warriors of Garellis will never be defeated."

Jezebelle smiled, holding Gerard close.

Boreas walked his horse right up to Jurien, "Release him."

The other warriors did so, following the orders of their new king.

"You are hereby exiled from the kingdom of Garellis," Boreas said, "Leave, and never return."

Jurien nodded, turning and running into the forests of Gliken.

Vega came back to reality, staring at the faces of Boreas, Byun, Thaan-dor, and Thrindil. Her headache intensified all over again, worse this time. Her nose began to bleed as she blacked out once more.

Thaandor

13

"Vega, come back to us," Thaandor's voice rang out in her mind. She felt a strange energy through her body as she regained consciousness. She realized Thaandor had been healing her, and giving her some of his energy to revive her.

"Sit slowly," he instructed, "How do you feel?"

"Terrible," she replied, her throat raspy. She could feel the dried blood sticking to her face, trailing from her nose to her chin.

"That's to be expected," Thaandor said, "Don't worry. You'll be alright." He turned to the others, "Thrindil, she needs something to eat and drink. Byun, fetch her a pillow and a blanket so she can rest. Boreas, I believe she's ready to speak with you."

As Thrindil and Byun hurried to fulfill his instructions, he gave Vega a pat, leaving her alone with Boreas.

"It's time for you to go," she said, "But there is something you must know. I know you won't like it, but you need to hear it to prepare yourself mentally for what awaits you."

He nodded, bracing himself.

"When you return, Jurien will be overthrown, and you will be the new king."

"What?" he said, shocked, "There must be some mistake. I'm not king material. Besides, who would vote for me?"

"Nearly the entire kingdom," she replied, "Thaddeus will nominate you, and Jezebelle will second his nomination. Gerard will call for a vote, and almost everyone will raise their hands. I knew you would be the new king back in Gliken, but I didn't think you were ready to hear it. I told Jezebelle, though, and that's why she voted for you. Or, I suppose, why she *will* vote for you."

Boreas sat shocked for a moment, contemplating.

"You will make a good king because you don't *want* to be king. You're not power-hungry like so many others. You care about your fellow elves, and they respect you for it. You were always destined to be king."

He gave a deep nod, lost in his thoughts.

"Thank you for bringing me here safely," Vega said, "You're a good man, Boreas. I shall miss your company."

"I shall miss you, too, young oracle," he replied, "You have changed my life. When you wake, I shall be gone, but you will always be in my heart, as well as my family's." He patted her shoulder, careful not to touch her skin again.

As he rose, Byun placed a pillow under her head and laid a blanket over her. Thrindil handed her a cup of water and a piece of chocolate. She ate it and drank it quickly, lying down and passing out as soon as her head hit the pillow.

When she woke, Boreas was gone, just as he'd said. She spent the day writing the scrolls she would send with Byun when she let him go. The slow, careful practice of calligraphy was relaxing for her—each stroke of her quill making satisfying marks on the paper before her.

It helped give her something mindless to focus on, so she could let her body heal and give her mind a much-needed break. With all the visions that had rattled her the day before, she wasn't sure she could stand another one. She couldn't even think about finding a keeper, or moving into her new house. All she wanted to do was put words on paper.

When she finished, she ate a large meal provided by Thrindil, who was off attending to council matters, and went back to sleep. Byun watched over her, finding ways to occupy himself around the house. Thaandor had returned to his house, as his work there was finished.

She spent the next day eating and napping, her body still trying to recover. She was glad her prophecy had come together, because she didn't think she could stand another vision anytime soon.

The following day was spent much the same. She also spent time doodling to occupy her mind. She was relieved to just be able to relax. It seemed like it had been a long time since she'd been able to do just that.

Finally, the next day, she felt well enough to begin walking around more. Byun helped her a bit, as she made her way around Thrindil's house. She even walked outside, making her way around the hills. It felt good to breathe fresh air in, and she was glad to have Byun's company. His narrow eyes closed as the breeze caressed his ivory cheek.

"Byun?" Vega asked.

"Yes, Vega?"

"Would you like to see my house?"

He nodded, "Maybe tomorrow. I think this is far enough for you today."

She sighed, "Very well."

The two of them headed back inside, much to Tabatha's disappointment. She had been bored the last few days, being cooped up in the house. Though she obviously cared for Vega, she was a pixie. She didn't belong indoors. She longed to be outside in the fresh air.

Soon, Vega thought, *You'll be free to fly around my house whenever you wish. I shall even plant a garden for you . . .*

Vega awoke to Byun shaking her gently, "There's someone here to see you."

She got up, confused, and headed into the main room of Thrindil's house. Thaandor was there, looking concerned.

"I wanted to check on you, and see how you were doing," he said, holding up a basket of cakes and cookies.

"I'm fine," she said, taking a seat on the burgundy couch, "Thank you for the concern."

"She walked around the hills yesterday," Byun said, "I think by tomorrow, she'll be back to normal."

"You endured a lot, taking on those visions," Thaandor said, sitting opposite her, "I've been worried about you."

Vega took a cookie from the basket he'd set on the table, taking a bite. It was warm and gooey, and she indulged in the sugar, hoping it would raise her energy level.

He smiled, "I thought these would put a smile on your face."

"It's been a long time since I've had any sweets," she replied.

"I think it's important to indulge occasionally," he said, "Sugar soothes the soul."

Vega laughed, "Who told you that?"

Thaandor chuckled, "It's one of my personal philosophies."

She smiled, enjoying the feeling of being able to have a conversation about things other than her visions.

"If she's going to make a full recovery," Byun interrupted, "she needs rest."

"I've rested enough," Vega said in irritation, "All I've been doing the last few days is resting. I'd like to have a normal conversation."

"Well, if you continue resting today, then by tomorrow, you should feel fine. If you try to push it, you'll only prolong your recovery."

As she opened her mouth to argue, Thaandor said, "That's alright. I should be going, anyway. Theodora's waiting for me. We have big plans tonight."

"Listen, Thaandor, about Theodora—" Vega began.

"Thaandor," Thrindil said, walking through the door, "What a pleasant surprise. What brings you to my house?"

"I was actually just leaving," he replied, "I merely stopped by to see how Vega was doing, and bring her some treats."

"Oh, well, bring Theodora by soon," he said, "I'd love to have you both for dinner."

"Of course," Thaandor said, nodding, "We'll see you very soon."

"I'll hold you to it," Thrindil replied.

When morning came, Vega felt refreshed. It had been a while since she'd actually felt that way when she woke up. She breathed deep, feeling like herself again. Unfortunately, that meant she actually had to think about the pressing matters in her life. She had her own house, but she still needed a keeper. She had to send Byun to deliver her prophecy to the dwarves, and to the village of Kataran. But she couldn't live by herself.

She wandered out to the main room, and saw that Byun was asleep on the couch. Thrindil was working. Tabatha was getting very claustrophobic, waiting on her to recover.

Today's the day, she thought, *I'm moving into my house.* The only problem with that was the matter of finding her a new keeper.

As soon as she'd thought it, there was a soft knock at the door. She hurried to answer it so as not to wake Byun. He'd been so busy fussing over her the last few days, he'd hardly slept. When she opened it, there stood Thaandor, looking utterly broken and forlorn.

He looked up at her with tears in his eyes, "Vega, I—"

"Come in," she said, holding the door open.

The old wizard entered, "I don't want to bother you. I'm not even sure why I'm here, to be honest."

"Theodora left you," she said.

He looked at her, "How'd you . . . you saw?"

She nodded, "I tried to tell you, but I just didn't know how."

He paused, "Is that what you discussed with her the day we met?"

Vega grimaced, "Yes. I saw her running away with Rigel. I didn't know who she was, or who he was. I wasn't sure what significance it held. So, I asked Thrindil to arrange a meeting with her. When she showed up with you, her fiancé . . . "

Thaandor nodded, "I get the picture."

"I'm sorry I didn't tell you. I tried to talk her out of it, but . . . "

He nodded again.

"I'm sorry."

"I wouldn't have believed you, anyway," Thaandor said, "Nobody could tell me anything about her."

Vega looked down.

"I have nothing," he said, "No wife, no family, no job . . . "

"I still have those sweets you brought," she said, trying to cheer him up, "They're good for the soul, remember?"

He looked down sorrowfully.

"You have me," she said, "I'll always be your friend."

Suddenly, Thaandor looked up at her, "That's it."

She shot him a confused look, "What's it?"

"That's why I'm here. Of course, it makes so much sense now . . . "

"What are you talking about?"

He looked at her, "Vega, I'd like to become your keeper."

"Whoa," she said, waving her hands at him, "As much as I would love that, it's very important not to make life-altering decisions after a loss."

"I understand that," he replied, "But, I'm serious. I've been searching for something meaningful to do with my long life, and after over two-hundred-and-fifty years, I still haven't. I think this is it. This is what I'm meant to do." He took her hands in his, "Vega, I'd like you to make me your new keeper."

Cabri

14

"If you want to be my keeper, you'll have to prove yourself," Vega said, "This can't be a fleeting whim to help you get over Theodora. You need to prove that you're committed to the job."

Thaandor nodded, "What do you need me to do?"

Just then, Byun stretched and yawned from the couch, waking up.

"Meet me at my house tomorrow afternoon, and I shall tell you," Vega said.

Thaandor gave a quick bow, turning and leaving before Byun could see him.

"Vega? You're awake!" Byun said, "How do you feel today?"

"I feel fine," she replied, "Actually, I feel better than I have in a long time."

"That's great!" he said.

She nodded, "I'd like to go to my house tomorrow."

Byun returned her nod, "Yes, if you're feeling this well today, I think it would be okay for you to go there tomorrow."

"Tabatha, did you hear that?" she called.

Her pixie friend flew into the room, twirling excitedly.

"We get to go home tomorrow, and I'm going to plant you a beautiful garden."

She darted back and forth, trailing pixie dust happily behind her.

"I think things are finally working out," Vega said, "Now that the prophecy is complete, I feel like I can focus on me again, and finally gain a permanent home."

The next morning, they said *goodbye* to Thrindil, heading to Vega's new home. They rode upon Byun's steed, Kimmi. Tabatha was a ball of energy, flying in circles beside Vega's head the whole way there. The elliptical, ivory structure was as she remembered, and she felt a sense of peace and comfort there. She showed Byun inside, as he marveled at the house she'd created.

"So, this is home to you, huh?" he asked.

She nodded.

"I've never seen anything like it, that's for sure. How'd you come up with it?"

"I modeled the color after Tabatha, and the shape is based on the sails of the ships I've seen in books. I always wanted to be on one, sailing somewhere very far away. Now, I can live inside my fantasy. The front room is perfect for readings, and the rest of the house is my personal, private sanctuary. Well, for me and Tabatha. And, I suppose, any actual guests."

Byun looked around again, "I hope you find happiness, Vega. I truly do."

"Thank you," she said, looking at him, "I'm sure you would make an excellent keeper. It's just that the evils of this world are too great. I must have someone powerful, who can defend me from them all."

He nodded, "I know. And, happy as I am to fill in, I've realized that I bit off more than I could chew, offering my services."

She paused, "Well, you won't have to much longer. I think I have found a new keeper. I have only to test his resolve."

Suddenly, her witch's glass began buzzing. She lifted it, saying, "Jezebelle?"

To her surprise, she saw B's face looking back at her, "It's me, Vega."

"B? How are you calling me?"

"We have a kingdom wizard, like many others. Anyway, I just called to thank you for sending me home. You were right. My family did have big news!"

Vega looked at him, puzzled. Boreas had told her B's son was only five. What "big news" was he referring to? "That's great," she said, not wanting to admit she hadn't foreseen whatever he was talking about.

"Do you want to meet her?" he asked.

Her confusion grew as she enthusiastically said, "Sure!"

He tilted the witch's glass so she could see his wife, Aura, holding a baby in her arms.

"I made it just in time!" he said, "Isn't she beautiful? Her name is Lucy."

Vega smiled, realizing he meant the birth of his daughter, "Yes, she is."

He kissed her forehead, and the three of them smiled and waved as their image faded from view, leaving the reflective surface of the witch's glass once more.

She felt good about sending the others home, and she knew everything was almost over. "Byun," she said, "I need you to watch the house for a few days."

He looked at her questioningly, "Why?"

"I need to go somewhere. I'll be back, but I trust you to watch the house."

"You didn't have anyone watching the house while you were staying with Thrindil," he said skeptically, "Why do you really want me to stay here?"

She sighed, "I'm going to test Thaandor, to see if he's truly committed and capable of being my new keeper. I just . . . didn't want to hurt your feelings."

"You won't," he replied, "I told you already; it's too much for me."

She nodded.

"Thaandor?" he asked.

Vega smiled, "Yes. I think he will make a good keeper, but I don't want him to agree to it for the wrong reasons, and back out later, or wish he had."

Byun nodded, "I understand. Good luck with your testing. I'll be content to stay here with Tabatha until you return. Perhaps I'll plant that garden for you. She can even help me."

At that, Tabatha fluttered over, looking eager. She sprayed a shower of pixie dust over Byun in appreciation and excitement.

"It looks like that's a yes," Vega said, laughing.

Just then, there was a knock at the door. She answered it, welcoming Thaandor inside.

He looked over at Byun uncertainly, "Hello, Byun."

"Hello, Thaandor," the black-bearded dwarf replied, matching his serious tone.

The old wizard looked uneasy, scratching his long, gray beard.

Vega laughed again, "It's alright, Thaandor. Byun already knows, and he's fine with it."

Byun chuckled, heading down the corridor to give them some privacy.

Thaandor appeared nervous, looking around the kitchen.

"We're going to the realm of the dragon riders," Vega said finally.

He shot her a questioning look.

"Who would be more powerful that you would have to protect me from than dragon riders?" she said, "Plus, it will test your diplomatic skills, as you facilitate our conversation. It's the perfect test."

He looked at her hesitantly.

"Or do you not feel like you can handle it?" she chided.

"No, no," he said quickly, "Let's go. What are we waiting for?"

Vega smiled, "Do you have a horse? Or shall we walk?"

Thaandor and Vega set out upon the back of Thaandor's white mare, Damask, leaving Tabatha and Byun at Vega's house. They rode all day, making it to the border between the wizard realm and the dragon rider realm. They stopped to make camp, staying on the wizard side for the night.

The open prairie didn't feel as safe at night, without the cover of trees to shield them from wandering eyes in the darkness. Vega nestled into the soft grass, trusting Thaandor to protect her. *I suppose this really will be a good test,* she thought.

The old wizard sat beside her, keeping watch as she slept. He was as stoic as a statue, and Vega began to trust him more, seeing his dedication to the task. Damask stood close by, loyal to her owner. She grazed on the grass, looking completely relaxed. The peaceful horse helped ease her worries. Her golden and amber hair made a soft cushion beneath her head, and the scents of the grass and flowers helped her drift off to sleep…

As the sun began to rise, they moved through the magical barrier between the realms, leaving behind the grassy plain, and entering the dry, hot, dusty desert of the dragon rider realm. There were mountains in the distance, and before them, the dragon rider city of Cabri. They could see dragons flying above it, far ahead, as they rode upon Damask.

When they reached the gate, the guards shouted, "Who goes there?"

"We are friends," Thaandor said, "We have come seeking an audience with your king."

They looked at each other, unsure. Finally, they opened the gate, allowing them inside. One of them began leading them through the city, to the gold and emerald palace at its peak. Vega marveled at seeing a real-life dragon for the first time up close. They were far larger than she could have imagined.

They were led inside the massive structure, and to the throne room. Upon the throne sat their queen, garbed in silver armor, with short, brown hair and silver eyes. Well, one silver eye. Her other eye was covered in a long scar that went from her scalp to her chin. A sleeping silver dragon lay next to her.

"Welcome, outsiders," she said, "I am Sarafin, queen of the riders. What brings you to our great city?"

"Not *Queen* Sarafin?" Thaandor asked.

She smirked, "I am the queen of the dragon riders. What more of a title do I need? We do not believe in addressing our royalty as King or Queen. When you command power such as ours, the fluffy titles are unnecessary."

"I see," he said, bowing, "Forgive my ignorance."

Sarafin rolled her eyes, "You have yet to answer the question. What brings you here?"

"This young lady is an oracle," he said, "She wishes to bestow a vision of the future upon you."

"An oracle, you say?" she said, looking at Vega curiously.

Thaandor nodded, "She would need to meet with you privately, as what she would say would be for your ears only."

"Very well," Sarafin said, "But, if this is some sort of trick, just know that my guards will be just outside the door. Though, I don't really need them. I can handle myself." She looked at her pointedly.

"Understood," he said, "It's no trick."

She rose, descending the steps from her throne. As she did, Vega couldn't help but notice her abnormally large backside. She averted her eyes quickly, waiting for her to stop before them.

"You may wait here, wizard," she said, turning to Vega, "You may follow me."

She trailed behind her as they exited the throne room, heading down a corridor. Sarafin led her into a small room—too small for a dragon—probably the smallest room in the castle. It had padded walls and a couple of large cushions in the center of the floor.

"Please, sit," she said, sitting on one of the cushions herself.

Vega sat opposite her on the other cushion.

"Shall we begin?" Sarafin asked.

She nodded, holding out her hands.

The queen of the riders placed her hands in hers, waiting patiently.

As she did, a vision came to Vega. She stood in the throne room, where the queen she'd seen in her previous vision of the riders stood. Sarafin was there as well, but she no longer wore a crown. She had a silver band around her head instead.

"Kirstiana, you cannot accept trades with the wizard realm," Sarafin said.

She smirked, "I can do what I wish. *I* am queen, not you. Or did you so quickly forget?"

"You are still my daughter," she replied, "And, as your mother, I forbid you to do this."

"*You* forbid *me*?" she said, laughing, "Not anymore." She met her gaze steadily, "I no longer take orders from the likes of you. All my life, you've ordered me around. Now that I am queen, you still want to micromanage my decisions. Well, I shan't allow it. The authority over this kingdom rests with me."

"You fool!" Sarafin shouted, "You put our people in jeopardy! This is bigger than your feelings about me."

"You're right," Kirstiana replied, "This is bigger than you and me. It's a huge change that will bring about opportunity and prosperity for our people. It's something you were never bold enough to do. But, I trust the wizards, unlike you. I do not believe they mean us harm by their offer of commerce."

"You are wrong," she said.

She stood tall and proud, "We'll see."

"Unfortunately, my daughter, in that you are correct."

The vision faded away, and Vega knew she could not tell Sarafin what she'd seen. She would have to tell her something, though. She kept her eyes closed, trying to pretend she was still having a vision, so as to avoid suspicion while giving her time to think about what to say.

"Well?" Sarafin asked, "What did you see?"

Vega dropped her hands, looking up at her, "Your daughter, Kirstiana, will be a fine queen one day. In fact, she will be instrumental to a prophecy of mine. It's still in the works, but I see a great future for her."

She scoffed, "That is what you see when you look into my future? Not me, but my daughter?"

She nodded, "I'm afraid I have no control over what I see. I only get whatever fragments of the future come to me."

"Why did you bother to come here at all, then?"

"I had visions of great importance in the other lands I've traveled to so far, including the dwarves' and the elves' territories. I thought perhaps I might here as well. Plus, I wished to test my new keeper's diplomacy skills in facilitating our conversation."

"And, how did he do?" she asked.

"You tell me."

Sarafin smirked, "You are smart, I'll give you that. I think he did well, especially considering it was his first interaction."

Vega nodded, "Good. I think he has what it takes, but I needed to be sure."

"As for my daughter, she's headstrong, stubborn, and naive. She would have us welcome in the outside world, but most of our people are old-school. We have learned from the mistakes of our past, and realize that welcoming them in is dangerous. It is better for us all if we remain apart, and take care of our own above all else. I'm not so convinced as you that she would make a good queen."

She was silent.

Sarafin sighed, "Come. Let us return to the throne room. I will grant you and your keeper room and board tonight. Tomorrow, you may set out back to where you came from."

Once she and Thaandor were settled in the guest suites—which Vega was excited about, as she'd never slept in a bed so large before, and she had the whole room to herself for once—they decided to wander a bit, exploring the massive, fascinating rooms of the dragon rider castle.

The west side of the castle had the guest rooms, the throne room, the library, and a hall of portraits of the past royals. The east side had a conference room, a massive arena, and a massive dining hall. The north side was restricted, with the private rooms of the royals, and the south side had shrines dedicated to recently fallen dragons and riders.

Vega marveled at the size of it all, though she knew it was designed so dragons could fit inside. There were several dragons and councilmen meandering through the castle, as well as servants bustling about. She'd never seen a place like it before. It was frighteningly impressive.

As the two of them were exploring the dining hall, she caught sight of a familiar face. Kirstiana was there with her dragon! The cooks were bringing out several roasted beasts for her dragon to eat.

"Thaandor," Vega said, "I want to talk to her."

The old wizard nodded, "Very well. Let's go."

They made their way over to her, stopping a short distance away. They dared not venture too close to a hungry dragon.

"Hello there," Thaandor called.

Kirstiana looked at them questioningly, "Can I help you?"

"Kirstiana?" Vega said.

She looked at her, even more perplexed. "Do I know you?" she asked.

"No," Vega replied, "But, I know you. Can we talk?"

She sized them up, her amber eyes wary. She brushed a strand of auburn hair from her face, nodding to her dragon. Then, she made her way to a nearby table, taking a seat. Thaandor and Vega followed, sitting across from her.

"I am an oracle," Vega began.

"She is *The* Oracle," Thaandor inserted.

"I have had visions of you," she continued, "And, I think I should share my latest one with you."

Kirstiana nodded suspiciously, "Very well." After a pause, she looked at the gray-bearded wizard, "Who's he?"

"He is my keeper," she said, "Don't worry. He's sworn to secrecy." She eyed Thaandor.

He quickly realized she was signaling him, and said, "Oh, yes. I won't tell a soul. I am bound to her, and she to me. I am a steward of the future."

Vega rolled her eyes. After a pause, she said, "I had a vision of you and your mother. You were queen. You wished to open trade with the wizard realm, and she opposed you."

Kirstiana let out a laugh, "Is that supposed to surprise me?"

"No," she said, "I figured it would sound about right. You held your own against her, though, and since the authority will rest with you, she couldn't overrule you."

"I know," she replied, "I look forward to that day."

"I fully support your plan," Vega said, "I told your mother nothing of it. I only said that you will make a great queen."

"Thank you," she said, surprised.

"That would be a wonderful idea!" Thaandor said, "Us wizards could use the trades. I'm sure we have things you desire, and vice versa. And, there are so many magical projects where we could use the help and strength of a dragon. The projects would be beneficial to both our realms. If we are to share Abyumo, let us share it!"

Kirstiana nodded enthusiastically, "Exactly! My mother is narrow-minded. She lives in the past. I want to lead us into the future. Our people should be part of the world, not secluded from it."

"I agree," he said, "It's been many years since riders involved themselves in the affairs of the world."

"Riders of old did, but not today," she said, shaking her head in disappointment, "I want to change that. But, it will be difficult to sway the council. Since it is the queen's job to take their opinions into account, I know I must build a rapport with them, and accept most of their decisions, even when I disagree. It will take time to establish change."

"That it will," he agreed, "It's a hard thing to do."

"Not to mention, my mother will fight me every step of the way," she continued, "She thinks it's dangerous for our people to get involved. But, what good is being a dragon rider if we're afraid of the rest of the world? What's life without a little risk?"

"Too true," he said, "Too many of us live our lives in fear. I have long believed dragon riders to be fearless. But now, I see that even they hold fears of their own."

Kirstiana shook her head, "This is the kind of reputation I want to avoid. Let not the rest of the world see cowards, hiding in their realm. Let them see the bravery and fearlessness of a nation that rides upon the backs of the world's most fearsome creatures!"

"It will take a great deal of strength, patience, and perseverance to achieve that goal," Thaandor replied.

She nodded, "Yes. Unfortunately, it will. I can only hope my future child will further that vision instead of destroying it."

"Perhaps I might be able to see that," Vega said.

Kirstiana looked at her uncertainly.

She held out her hands, waiting for her to take them.

She looked back and forth between the two of them, unsure whether she should. But, eventually, her curiosity won, and she grasped her hands.

Nothing happened. Vega was disconcerted, wanting to give her a message, but seeing nothing. Then, suddenly, the vision came. *Just a reminder that they appear in their own good time,* she thought.

She saw a queen with flowing, brown hair and bronze eyes. She was riding upon a bronze dragon, leading an army of riders into battle. As she looked at the battlefield below, she saw humans, dwarves, elves, wizards, and even kodrizans fighting. The races weren't segregated, but all fighting together. Kirstiana rode up beside her, "Lorena! Are you ready?"

She nodded, "Yes, mother. Let us fight!"

The two of them flew ahead together, meeting with their enemies.

As the vision shifted, she saw Kirstiana and Sarafin. The latter was old—her short hair gray, and her voluptuous backside sagging. She limped over to her bed, lying down. She looked sick.

"Are you alright, mother?" Kirstiana asked.

"Back off!" Sarafin shouted, shooing her.

She sighed, frustrated.

"You destroyed this realm, and everything I worked my whole life for. I lived just long enough to see it. And now . . . now your daughter—my granddaughter—is following in your footsteps."

Kirstiana stood tall and proud, "Good. She will lead us into a new age. Thanks to my efforts, and now hers, our people will have a bright future. I am proud to call her my daughter."

"Well, I'm ashamed," Sarafin replied, "I'm ashamed of you both. You have ruined what we had—what our ancestors built. My reign was the end of an era."

"Yes," she said, "It was."

The vision faded away, and Vega was left saddened by the exchange. Though she was pleased to see Kirstiana's vision come to fruition, she was disheartened that she and her mother would never reconcile. She knew she couldn't help that, either. If she were to tell Sarafin what she'd seen, she would never allow her daughter to take the throne. There was nothing she could do to convince her. And she knew telling Kirstiana wouldn't help, as it was Sarafin who needed to forgive her, and not the other way around.

She sighed, saying, "Good news or bad news?"

The future queen blinked in surprise, looking at her with apprehension. Finally, she said, "Bad news."

"You and your mother will never reconcile. Even on her deathbed, she will hold you a grudge."

She sighed, disheartened, "I hadn't expected anything less of her. Though, I had still hoped." After a pause, she asked, "What's the good news?"

"Your daughter, Lorena, will continue your mission, making it a reality."

"Lorena?" she asked, "That's what I name her?"

Vega nodded, "That's what you called her in my vision."

"I'm going to have a daughter?" she asked in amazement.

She nodded again.

After a long pause, she said, "Thank you. The two of you have helped give me hope for the future, and reassurance that I'm doing the right thing."

They both nodded.

"I'd better get back to Solstra," she said, "She gets restless after a feeding."

"Solstra?" Vega asked, "That's your dragon's name?"

She nodded.

"It's beautiful," Thaandor said, "The perfect name for an amber dragon."

Kirstiana laughed, "I like to think so." She walked over to her dragon, mounting her, and they took off, up through the skylight.

A New Keeper

15

When Vega went to sleep that night, she had another vision. Kirstiana was being crowned queen. As she descended the steps to the party in her honor, Sarafin embraced her. Vega was extremely confused by the exchange. *I thought they never reconciled,* she thought.

Then, she saw her walk over to Thaandor.

"The Oracle sends her congratulations," he said.

She smiled, hugging him, "Thank you for everything, Thaandor."

"It was my pleasure," he replied.

"If it weren't for you talking to my mom on my behalf, we would never have put aside our differences."

He blushed, "Well, I can't take all the credit. I was only doing my duty as The Oracle's keeper."

"Still, thank you," Kirstiana smiled, "I owe you. If you ever need anything, you need only come to me."

"Thank you," Thaandor said, "And I shall continue to be there for you, not only as your liaison with the wizards and The Oracle, but as your friend."

She smiled again, "I count you highly among my own friends as well. You will always be welcome here."

As the vision faded away, Vega realized that Thaandor would make an excellent keeper, and that he would serve as a fine ambassador for the outside world. She had only the problem of paying him for his services. She needed money as well, if she were going to eat and otherwise provide for herself. *How can I possibly make an income?* she wondered.

As the sun peeked in through the window, she and Thaandor got up, readying to set out. Part of her would miss traveling to other lands, but part of her wanted nothing more than to rest and relax in the comfort of her own home. When she thought of home, thoughts of her parents floated through her mind. She hoped they were doing well, in spite of her leaving. She knew they were probably deeply saddened by her departure. She never wanted to hurt them. She simply couldn't stay in Kataran and become slave to the council. Being an oracle was full of hard decisions.

As she and Thaandor climbed upon Damask's back, a vision came to her. She saw her parents, sitting in their house, looking morose as they went about their daily activities. Her father struggled to plow their field, and her mother sat in her chair knitting, instead of socializing with the other villagers. It was hard for her to watch, as she thought that this pain had been caused by her.

Then, it shifted, and she saw them again. They looked a bit older now, but not quite gray. Her father was eating breakfast. Her mother was just coming down the stairs. "Dale?" she said.

"Yes, Lenore?" he asked, not looking up from his plate. When she didn't respond, he looked up.

She suddenly nodded, nearly bursting into tears with excitement.

"Are you pregnant?" he asked, getting up.

She nodded again, tears flowing down as they embraced. After a pause, she said, "We have a second chance, Dale. We're gonna have a baby."

He wrapped his arms around her in hope and disbelief.

The vision shifted again, and she saw her mother holding a baby in her arms. Her father was standing beside her, and they were both looking lovingly down at the infant. They looked far happier than she had seen them in a long time.

"Welcome home, Jacob," Lenore said, kissing him on the forehead.

"Yes," Dale said, "Welcome home, son."

The vision shifted one last time, and she saw her brother, a young child. He was running through the streets of Kataran, playing with the other children. He looked perfectly normal. There was nothing wrong with him. He was not an oracle.

Just then, her mother appeared in the doorway of their house, "Jacob! Time for dinner!"

The young boy with brown hair and eyes like their parents turned, seeing Lenore standing there. He said *goodbye* to his friends, running back toward the house. Their mother opened the door, smiling broadly as she watched him run inside. Dinner was on the table, and Dale was seated at the head. He beamed when Jacob ran inside, happy to see his son coming home for dinner.

As the vision faded away, Vega felt bittersweet. She was glad to see her parents found happiness, and got the lives they always wanted. They had become residents of their new village in Katangalo, and they finally had a normal child, and one who wouldn't run away.

On the other hand, she felt like they had replaced her. She felt like she didn't mean that much to them, since they were able to just have another kid and move on. She was jealous of her brother for being able to have a normal life. She felt like that should have been her life, but it had been stripped away from her.

On top of all that, she felt guilty for feeling resentful. They had lost everything when she left, and it was selfish of her to deny them their happiness. A tear rolled down her cheek, and she wasn't sure if it was a sad tear or a happy tear. Maybe it was both, a result of all the mixed-up emotions she was feeling.

In any case, she was glad to know what became of them, and to see them smiling and living their lives, not dwelling in their sorrow over her. They were able to move on. And, so would she. She was ready to begin her new life as The Oracle. She needed only to establish a source of income for both herself and her keeper. And, that was harder than it seemed.

As she and Thaandor rode back to the wizard realm, she began to think of how she could manage it. Should she charge people for her visions? That didn't seem right to her. Yet, she thought she could always tell people for free when it would affect kingdoms, countries, or the world. She could charge people who came to her seeking a reading for their own purposes . . .

Would that be enough? she thought, *How many people would be willing to travel to Abyumo, in the realm of the wizards, simply to hear a reading?*

When her house became visible again, she noticed an ivory glow coming from within. She stared at it curiously, wondering what was causing it. As she dismounted Damask, opening the doors, she was blinded by a bright light and gust of wind. When it died down, she saw that Tabatha had been the cause. She was dancing upon a shelf in the corner of the front room, her pixie magic causing pulses of wind and light.

"I should always have you in here when visitors come for a reading," she said, "It was magical and mysterious when I opened the doors."

On hearing her voice, Tabatha excitedly darted over, circling her head and nearly getting caught in her hair.

"It's good to see you, too," Vega said, "Did you and Byun plant the garden?"

The tiny, ivory pixie darted toward the door to the rest of the house, and she and Thaandor followed. When they got inside, they saw that Byun was cooking dinner. He was singing and dancing as he pulled a casserole from the oven. When he saw the two of them, he let out a yell, nearly throwing the dish.

"Vega! Thaandor! You're back!" he yelled, "You scared me."

Vega laughed, "I see that. Thanks for keeping the house intact for me, Byun. Tabatha was just showing me the way to the garden you planted together."

"Oh, yes," he said, "I'm sure you'll love it. I've just made dinner. There should be enough for all of us."

"Great," she replied, "Thank you, Byun!"

Tabatha flitted around her head again, gaining her attention. They continued to follow her through the back door. Behind the house, and along the windowsills, was a beautiful little garden. It was covered in vibrant, sweet-smelling flowers, and Vega was thrilled with how it had come out. It was the perfect place for her pixie friend to live, and she knew she would be happy, too, now. She wouldn't have to stay cooped up in the house all day, but have instead a place she could go to breathe the fresh air, and wallow in the plants.

"It's beautiful!" Vega said, "It's perfect."

Tabatha twirled around in delight.

"It truly is the perfect place for you to call home," Thaandor said, "I'm very happy for you."

The three of them went back inside, eating dinner with Byun, enjoying his cooking, and his company.

When they were finished, Vega said, "Thaandor, I'd like to officially offer you the job of becoming my keeper."

He smiled, "Of course, Vega. I accept."

She returned his smile, happy to finally have a home and a keeper. Then, she turned to Byun, "You are free to go, Byun. You may return home to your people. Just don't forget about delivering the prophecy to Kataran as well as Dirthix."

The black-bearded dwarf nodded, smiling all the way to his narrow eyes, "I shall fulfill your requests. I am both happy and relieved to be able to finally return to the dwarven tunnels."

They all cleaned up together, enjoying more of each other's company that evening before Thaandor went home, and Vega and Tabatha went to their new room to go to sleep. Byun went to sleep in the guest room, preparing to set out the following morning.

As her pixie friend curled up on her little bed, Vega curled up in hers, finally happy. Everything was working out for her, and her new life was everything she could have hoped for.

In the morning, Byun set out, and Thaandor came over to begin his work as her keeper. Vega wasn't sure what to have him do, exactly. She still wasn't even sure how she could pay him. It occurred to her that she may have to go with her plan to charge people for readings. The only problem was letting people know she was there, and getting them to come to her. She needed to market herself somehow, and she had no idea how to do that.

"Thaandor?" she asked, "If you would like to earn a living as my keeper, I have your first assignment."

"Oh?" he said, curious, "And what's that?"

"I need you to travel around to the other lands, building a rapport with people, and getting them to come to me for readings. I can charge for my visions, and we can split the profits to support ourselves."

He sighed, rubbing the back of his neck, "I suppose we must, or we shan't make a living."

"I won't charge those involved in prophecies," she said, "Or those I request to speak with to avoid mass tragedy. But, for those who wish to come here and have me view their future, we must charge. The only question is: how much for a reading?"

"I think we could charge thirty pounds," he replied.

"That seems a bit high," Vega said, "How about twenty?"

"You are The Oracle," Thaandor said, "A reading from you is worth more than your average oracle. I say twenty-five."

She nodded, "Very well. Twenty-five it is."

"I shall go out and promote your ability," he said proudly. After a pause, he deflated, saying, "But, how am I to go out and send people here? If I am gone, who will protect you?"

Vega sighed, realizing he was right.

After a long pause, Thaandor said, "I have an idea." With that, he turned and walked out the door.

She looked at Tabatha, confused. After a moment, she hurried out the door to follow him. She saw him speaking with the council through a mirror.

"It's time," he said.

"You're actually willing to do it now?" Thrindil asked.

He nodded, "It's for Vega."

The other council members nodded.

"Very well," Thrindil said, "I shall summon the others."

Vega stared in confusion as the council's image faded from the mirror's surface.

"What are you willing to do?" she asked, coming out from her hiding spot behind her house.

Thaandor looked at her, "I'm going to help the council and Abyumo's most powerful wizards to construct a magical barrier around Abyumo. It will prevent anyone with ill intent from crossing into our realm."

Her eyes widened, "That's possible?"

He nodded.

"Then, why were you unwilling to do it before? And why do they need you?"

He sighed, "It's extremely taxing and dangerous. There's a risk we could all be killed constructing it. That's why we need so many wizards.

We can share the burden of the energy drain. But, it's still a risk, and one I wasn't willing to take before. I fear it may be necessary now, since I must leave you. It will ensure that you remain safe in my absence."

"No," she said, shaking her head, "If you die, along with so many other wizards, there will be no one to protect me at all. Besides, I won't let you risk it. I care too much."

"It's not up to you, Vega," he replied softly, "I've already agreed. The reason they need me is that I invented the spell."

"You . . . what?" she said in disbelief, "You invented the spell?"

He nodded, "It was small-scale when I did it. It almost killed me, even then. The others wanted to know how I'd created such a barrier around my house. When I told them, they wanted me to help them do it on a larger scale. I told them it was too uncontrollable, and we'd risk many deaths if we ever attempted it. The entire council volunteered, along with many of our most powerful wizards. We would have to coordinate with everyone around the land, and all do it at the same time. But, we'd never have enough to make it safe." He paused, "Now, I feel that it is necessary. The council is coordinating the other volunteers, and we're going to create this barrier."

"You were right not to do it before!" she cried, "Think of all the lives you're putting at risk!"

"All will be well, young oracle," he said, "With so much power aiding the spell, I am certain it shall be fine."

"And what if it's not?"

He sighed, "Then I was never meant to be your keeper."

The Oracle

16

Vega sat in her meditation room the entire day, trying to clear her mind. She was worried for her keeper, and she didn't want to lose another one. She disagreed strongly with his plan to construct a magical wall around Abyumo. Not because she thought having a magical barrier of protection was a bad thing, but because of the risk it posed to the wizards who would conjure it, including Thaandor.

Tabatha kept her company, flitting about the empty room, and sometimes going to her shelf, where they had placed a lantern shell with a miniature lounge room where the candle used to be. Now, the pixie could light it up when she went inside to relax.

The barrier was to be constructed the following morning, when they could get all the other wizards together to do it. Thaandor was back at his house, preparing. Vega was trying to figure out how to stop him, but she knew she couldn't. Even if she had a vision that they were all going to die, she knew he wouldn't listen, as he believed this barrier worth dying for. It would keep out anyone with ill intent, making the land of Abyumo safe for all its inhabitants, at least in the wizard realm.

She sighed, unable to focus on her meditation. She and Tabatha went to the garden, enjoying the sweet scents of the flowers, the fresh air in their lungs, and the beauty of the world around them. She wondered whether her life would ever feel even somewhat normal. From the moment she was born, it had been full of challenges and suffering. Just when she thought she could have a life, everything went downhill. *If he makes it through this,* she thought, *I think I'll finally get what I want . . .*

The next morning, Vega awoke to a loud humming sound. Her entire house was shaking, as though there was an earthquake. She scrambled out of bed, dressing quickly, and ran outside, her pixie friend trailing behind her. When she got there, she gawked in amazement at the sight before her. Thaandor and Thrindil were ahead, some distance apart, a shimmering silver wall of magic spreading from their staffs. She could see other witches and wizards in the distance, all standing at the border of Abyumo. Before her eyes, it spread, going out and up. The force of so much magic being used at once was the cause of the ground shaking. As it radiated out from each wizard, it merged with the next one's wall, until they all became one.

Vega's eyes widened at the beauty of the shimmering barrier they were creating. Once they had merged together, it went up for miles, to a point no one would be able to climb, jump, or launch themselves over. She thought they would be finished once the barrier was formed, but they kept going, and she could see it becoming stronger and thicker.

It began to take its toll on those conjuring it, and they struggled to keep going, trying to maintain their streams of magic. A couple of them dropped in the distance, and Vega worried that they were dead. Thrindil began to wobble, his knees buckling. Thaandor let out a yell as he tried to keep going. She could see that more weight had been put on him when the others had dropped.

Vega gasped, panicking. She wasn't sure what she could do. *Nothing,* she thought, *I can't do anything. I can't wield magic. I can't help him.* She looked down sorrowfully.

Suddenly, they all released their hold on the barrier, collapsing. As she looked, she could see that they had done it. The barrier was formed, and remained in place when they released the spell.

"Thaandor!" she shouted, rushing to his side.

He looked up at her, "It is done."

"I see," she said, "More importantly, are you alright?"

He nodded, practically whispering, "I will be."

She helped him up, putting his arm over her shoulders, and walked him to her house. She took him to the guest room, laying him down on the bed. She let out a sigh of relief once she got him there, saying, "Get some rest. I'll get you some food later."

He nodded, drifting off.

Once she'd taken care of Thaandor, she hurried back outside, going over to Thrindil, "Are you alright?"

He was sitting on the ground, breathing heavily. He couldn't even muster a reply, except to nod.

"Let me help you," she said, putting his arm over her shoulders and helping him up, "I gave my guest room to Thaandor, and I'm afraid I don't have a couch. But my front room is padded, with a cushioned floor, so it's comfortable to lie on."

He nodded again, struggling to remain upright.

She took him inside, laying him on the floor, "I'll get you a blanket and pillow. I'll bring you some food later."

He didn't reply, starting to wheeze.

She hurried inside, fetching him a blanket and pillow, and brought it to him. She slipped the pillow under his head and put the blanket over him. His coughing had gotten worse, so she hurried back inside, fetching him a glass of water.

When she brought it to him, he drank it gratefully, stopping his cough. Finally, he was able to lie down, drifting off to sleep.

Vega breathed a sigh of relief that she had been able to help them, but she was worried for all the others who had created the barrier. She wanted to help them, but she didn't have enough blankets and pillows for all of them. Plus, she remembered that there were enough of them to span the border of Abyumo. She didn't have the space, energy, or time to get to all of them. She could only do so much. She went back inside to get something the two wizards could eat when they woke.

Vega checked on them a few times to see if they were awake enough to eat. But, the two wizards remained asleep for the next two days. She began to worry they wouldn't wake at all. The food she'd prepared was cold, but she wasn't sure when or if she'd have need of it. She spent her time doodling, gardening, and checking on them.

Finally, Thrindil stirred. She hurried to heat some food for him, grabbing him another glass of water. When she returned to her front room, he was sitting up, looking around.

"Here," she said, offering the plate and glass, "Eat this."

He looked at her, dazed and confused. Finally, he took the plate, starting to shovel the food in.

She set the glass down beside him, saying, "I'm going to go check on Thaandor. If you're awake, he might be, too." She left Thrindil to eat and drink, going to her guest room. He was still passed out, unmoving. She sighed, returning to the front room. She was worried for her keeper, but she had hope, now that Thrindil was awake.

When she opened the door, he was finished eating. He looked up at her, "Thank you, Vega."

She nodded, coming into the room, "How are you feeling?"

"I'll be alright," Thrindil replied, "How long was I asleep?"

"Two days," she said.

He started to stand up.

"No," she said quickly, "Don't try to stand, yet. You need to take it easy."

He stood anyway, looking at her, "If I only just awoke, what of all the others?"

Vega was silent, unsure.

"I must find them and check on them," he said, "I thank you for helping me and Thaandor. But, there are many more who are perhaps in need of help. As head councilman, it is my duty to help them."

She nodded reluctantly, understanding.

With that, Thrindil headed out, going off to search for the other witches and wizards who were affected by the spell.

Vega grabbed the pillow and blanket he'd been using, throwing them in the laundry. As she was loading them into the washer, she heard a noise in the guest room. Her eyes widened, and she quickly prepared a plate of food and glass of water, bringing them in.

Thaandor was awake, stumbling around the room in confusion.

She set the food down on the nightstand, shouting, "Thaandor!"

He turned to look at her, glaze clearing from his eyes.

"It's alright; just take it easy. Have a seat. I brought you some food and water," she helped him to the bed to sit, handing him the plate.

He began eating, asking, "How long?"

"Two days," she replied, feeling as though she were having the same conversation twice.

As soon as he finished shoveling the food into his mouth and gulping down the water, he jumped up, saying, "I must go help the others."

Vega gently pushed him back, "Thrindil already went to help them. They'll be alright. Right now, I'm worried about you."

"I'm alright, thanks to you, Vega," he said gently, "But, there are many others who may not be. That barrier took a toll on everyone who aided its construction. Thrindil will not be able to help them all himself."

She sighed, looking down.

"I'll be alright," he said, "Thank you for helping me. I shall return; don't worry."

She nodded weakly.

With that, he hurried out the door, and she was left alone.

A couple more days went by before there was a knock at her door. When she answered, Thaandor stood before her.

"Hello, Vega," he said, "Sorry it took so long."

"That's alright," she replied, "You and Thrindil were right to help the others. I'm just glad you're alright."

He nodded.

She opened the door further, inviting him in, "Tabatha kept me company. I've been able to do a lot of studying and reading. I've learned new things about being an oracle."

"I'm setting out the day after tomorrow," he said suddenly.

She looked at him in confusion.

"I'm beginning the campaign trail to bring you customers. You're safe now, with the new barrier around the realm. I feel comfortable enough leaving you here, now."

"Why don't you wait a bit longer, to ensure you're recovered?" she asked.

"We need the money," he replied, "Neither of us can afford to feed ourselves without it much longer. The campaign will take a while. I need to get started as soon as possible. The council is still checking on all the other witches and wizards who helped us create the barrier. I got to as many as I could the last couple of days, but it's time to leave the rest to them. I've been caring for myself as well, don't worry. I feel much better after eating, drinking, and getting plenty of rest."

Vega sighed, "Alright. Just make sure you really are taking care of yourself. You are right about the money, but I think we could spare a couple extra days if it meant getting you back to full strength."

Thaandor smiled, "I appreciate the concern. But, you need not worry about me. I know how to take care of myself. The spell took a lot out of me, but I feel myself again, now. I have methods to recover my strength." He winked at her.

Though she didn't know what he was talking about, she returned his smile. She felt a bit better, knowing he was able to make a fast recovery in whatever fashion he meant. She supposed it was something to do with magic. As he'd said before, it was better not to ask questions. If she was meant to know, she would find out. Just then, she thought of something. In her vision where she was speaking with Nastazya, she had told her Nazir-dok had other sources of energy and strength. *I wonder if Thaandor is able to do the same,* she thought.

A couple of weeks went by, and she was beginning to develop a routine. She would spend the morning gardening with her pixie friend, then bathe and eat lunch. Then, she cleaned the house and spent a few hours studying, trying to learn all she could. She'd borrowed books from both Thaandor and Thrindil. After dinner, she would read for leisure, and then go for a walk through the hills with Tabatha. For another brief moment in life, she was happy. She felt a semblance of normality. Her twelfth birthday had come and gone, and she was another year older, another year wiser. She hoped this new year would mean a fresh start, and an end to the turbulence she'd endured over the last year.

One day, as she was busy studying dragons, there was a knock on her door. She went to answer it, and a peasant woman with a baby in her arms stood before her.

"Please, help me," she said, "My husband is sick. I need you to view my future to see if he will get better."

Vega wasn't sure how to react to this unexpected visitor. Her mouth opened and shut, and she couldn't think for a moment. Suddenly, she realized she had probably come because of Thaandor. This was her first customer. She cleared her throat, saying, "Certainly. Not to be a stickler, as I'm sure you've traveled very far, but I'm afraid there is a fee of twenty-five pounds for a reading."

The woman nodded, pulling the money from her pocket and handing it to her.

She took it in surprise, tucking it into the folds of her dress. After a pause, she said, "Please, come in." Vega took a seat in the center of the room, waiting.

The woman took a seat opposite her, situating the baby in her lap.

She took a breath, taking her hands, and hoping a vision would actually come to her. It did, and she was standing in a small cottage. The woman was there, walking through the door with her baby. There was a man lying in the bed. At first, she thought that he was sick, but then she realized he was dead. Vega reacted with horror, not wanting to tell this woman her husband wasn't going to make it.

When she opened her eyes, the woman was staring at her hopefully.

Vega blinked, looking sorrowful.

Suddenly, the woman's eyes filled with tears, "He's been sick a long time. I didn't think he was going to make it." She clutched the baby to her chest, "Now I know I must find a source of income for my daughter and I. Thank you for at least giving me an answer."

Before Vega could respond, the woman got up, heading out of her house. She sat there a long time, feeling devastated for this woman she didn't even know. She began to meditate, trying to level out her emotions. Suddenly, there was another knock at the door.

She got up warily to open it. A young man stood before her. "Yes?" she said.

"Are you The Oracle?" he asked.

"Yes."

He looked her up and down skeptically, taking in her peasant's dress. "You don't look like an oracle," he said finally.

"Have you come for a reading?" she asked, annoyed.

When he looked at her glowing white eyes, he nodded, handing her a stack of money.

She took it, counting it quickly. It was twenty-five pounds. She gave him a nod, inviting him in. They sat, and she took his hands, trying to summon a vision of the future. Nothing came to her. She looked at him, "Is there a question, in particular, you are trying to answer?"

"Yes," he said, "I want to know if there is greatness in my future. I have hopes of becoming a dragon rider. I want to know if an egg will hatch for me, or if I'll be stuck a poor farm boy forever."

Vega sighed, realizing why a vision hadn't come to her, "I'm afraid I see nothing out of the ordinary in your future."

He looked down, disappointed.

"But, remember, I only see your future if you continue on your current path. If you veer from that path, anything is possible. It's always possible to *change* the future."

He looked at her disgustedly, "What did I pay you for? Anyone could tell me I can change the future. That's the same thing as telling me you don't know! What a waste."

Vega stared at him, surprised. She hadn't expected such a negative reaction. As he got up to leave, she said, "Don't be angry with me for trying to soften the blow. I only wished to make you feel better. But, since you put it that way, enjoy your ordinary, boring life!"

He glared back at her before slamming the door behind him.

She let out a breath, irritated. *Being an oracle is not all it's cracked up to be*, she thought. She looked down at her brown peasant's dress, sighing in reluctant agreement, *I think it's time I start dressing the part, if I am to be The Oracle.*

Taking her recently acquired fifty pounds, Vega went to the nearby market. Almost all the clothing for sale consisted of wizard robes. Finally, she found a clothing stand selling garments for nomads. Hanging on the end of the stand was a turquoise crop top with sheer sleeves and turquoise pants with sheer legs. She bought that, along with a purple dress and a pink nightgown to wear around the house when she wasn't busy with customers seeking her visions. Though she knew she would grow over the years, she also knew she could have a replica of her vision ensemble tailored in a larger size.

She decided to offer her services only during certain hours, so she could enjoy just lounging around her home without someone knocking on her door. She headed back, creating an hours sign to post on her door. She would read futures from dawn until lunchtime, excepting special appointments, made by either herself or her keeper.

Then, she could eat, and have the rest of the day to spend with her pixie friend and/or her keeper. She could spend her time gardening, reading, studying, and otherwise enjoying her life, vision-free. That was the most important part for her: that she could have a life outside of her visions. She wasn't going to let them rule her. They were part of her job now, not her whole life.

As she was putting her new clothes in her wardrobe, she was struck with a vision. She saw the castle in Khanjgi, and an orb rolling across the floor. It was beautiful, mysterious, and dangerous. There was something wrong about it. It had a darkness to it. It rolled to the feet of a mysterious man with brown hair and dark eyes. She'd never seen him before. When he touched the orb, she watched him transform.

Before her stood Nazirdok. She gasped in horrified surprise and disbelief. He laughed maliciously, taking over the kingdom once more. He waited, not so patiently, for the stars to align again. Over the years, he developed a massive reserve of energy, beyond what he had previously been able to. When he conducted his ritual this time, there was no one who could stop him. His darkness spread, countless innocents dying in its wake.

Finally, at the turn of the century, a princess was born who could stop him. She was born so powerful, even his energy stores couldn't help him. Unfortunately, it was too much power for any one person to contain. As soon as she'd thwarted his ritual, her own powers destroyed her, ripping her body apart with the force of her magic.

What? Vega thought in disbelief, *I thought the prophecy was supposed to prevent this.*

The vision shifted, and she saw the moment Celestia thwarted Nazirdok's ritual. When he summoned his powers to him after she flipped the table, his ritual claimed him. She watched carefully as his body dissolved, his powers swirling around Celestia. When the starlight penetrated the room, it didn't obliterate his powers, as she'd previously believed. Instead, his powers retreated, trying to find a safe place to hide. They darted inside his crystal ball, preserving his powers even after his body had been destroyed.

She gasped, "Then, this whole prophecy is for nothing!"

Her vision shifted again, and she saw Bridgot, Celestia, and Kgansten. They looked older than they had before. She could see that Bridgot and Celestia were king and queen now. Thaandor was with them, along with a dark elven woman who looked familiar. It took her a moment to realize that it was Xharia—Kamine's older sister.

They were at the castle in Khanjgi. Through the skylight, they could see a star fall. As it did, Thaandor cast a spell over the orb. Vega noticed that he was using a wand, rather than his staff. Kgansten swung his axe down upon it. Xharia shot it with an arrow. Bridgot stabbed it with his sword. Celestia plunged a strange object into it. As she did, it was destroyed, along with Nazirdok's powers within it.

She finally realized what the object had been: a dragon talon! She pondered what she'd seen in wonder, realizing they could destroy his powers, and thus, truly fulfill her prophecy. But, as she thought of having Thaandor call Jezebelle and Byun so she could tell them, the vision shifted again. She was standing in a human castle.

"Where are you going, Bridgot?" Celestia asked.

"I can't take it anymore!" he cried, "I never knew royal life would be *this* restrictive! Now I know why you ran away! If I don't get out of here, I'm going to go crazy."

"What are you saying?" she asked, "You're leaving our family?"

He sighed, "I love you, Celestia. I love our kids. But this is all just too much! We've lost something . . . something we had before. I just don't think we can ever get it back. We've changed since our time on the quest of the prophecy."

"No," she said, tears in her eyes, "*You've* changed."

Vega watched with great sadness, realizing the two of them had been brought together by her prophecy, but time would drive them apart. It shifted again, and she saw the two of them sitting with Thaandor.

"My adventurous spirit has not died," Celestia said, "It is simply satisfied. I know my place and my duty to my people and my family. That is where my heart is. I've had my fill of adventure for the next hundred years after that one. I'm happy with what I have, and I'm ready to go home."

"Me, too," Bridgot said, "I thought I wanted a life of adventure, but really, I just needed another quest to quench my thirst. I thought we'd lost something after our last quest, but we didn't. It was simply suppressed for the time being. I thought life was boring and mundane, but I've grown to appreciate the peace of everyday life. We've fought hard enough for it. We've earned it. I think I'll be satisfied for the next hundred years as well."

Celestia smiled, "Glad to hear it."

He grasped her hand, "No matter how routine our life becomes, I don't think I could ever be bored with you."

As it shifted again, Vega realized if they destroyed the orb right away, their marriage would eventually die. But, if they waited, they would have a second quest to destroy it, and it would save their marriage. Considering the risk involved in leaving his powers in existence, she wasn't sure if it was worth it.

She saw her older self, Princess Celestia standing before her. "Once you've thwarted his ritual, you will find an orb amongst his ritual objects. It will contain his powers. In order to truly destroy him, you must destroy his powers," she said, "You can only do that with a weapon and warrior from each the five races of human, elf, dragon rider, wizard, and dwarf."

It shifted a seventh time, and she saw Celestia, Bridgot, and Kgansten standing in the aftermath of the ritual.

Celestia burst into tears, "After all that, now we have to destroy his powers, too. The Oracle said we need a weapon and warrior from each of the five races, and I could stand in for any one, as the princess of the prophecy. We had all five. But now, Aurano and Nastazya are gone."

Bridgot put his hand on her shoulder, comforting her, "We'll figure it out."

"No," she said, sobbing, "It's hopeless. We barely made it here. Now, we must find all these weapons, and try to gain two warriors after theirs were killed. Which of the races will be willing to grant us another?"

Kgansten and Bridgot hung their heads.

"Why did anyone think we could do this?" she asked, "There's no way."

"We have to try," Bridgot said softly.

"It may not mean much now," Kgansten said, "But, you still have me."

Celestia looked up hopefully, sighing, "You're right. We have to try."

The vision shifted again, showing flashes of the three of them trying to gather the warriors and weapons. Before they could even reach the riders, the orb was stolen in the night. Nazirdok's powers transplanted themselves into their new owner, and the dark wizard returned. With inky, menacing eyes, and sharp fangs grinning, he found the three of them. As they slept, he slaughtered them.

"No!" Vega yelled, feeling hopeless. Then, she realized she needed to wait to tell them about the second part of the prophecy until they were ready. When they first would go to thwart his ritual, they wouldn't be ready to destroy his powers yet. They would need Thaandor and Xharia to go with them to destroy the crystal ball.

More importantly, they needed a break in between quests. They needed time to get their lives back to normal. The elves and the riders needed time to mourn their fallen warriors before granting them another. Plus, the timing of the second quest—after their lives got boring—would save the marriage of the two biggest players in her prophecy.

They would only succeed if she waited to tell them. If she told them too soon, Nazirdok would return, and kill them before they were able to destroy his powers.

A New Home

17

Celestia wandered the displays in The Wizarding Museum, searching for something. Bridgot, Kgansten, and Thaandor followed, watching her intently. They were waiting on her to find what they were looking for. She rounded a corner, walking straight up to a wand in a glass case.

As she reached out to touch it, Thaandor shouted, "Don't!" But, it was too late. She placed her hands on the glass case. He drew nearer, staring at her in amazement, "How did you do that?"

"Do what?" she asked, breaking out of her trance.

"These cases are protected by magic."

"I'll say," Kgansten grumbled.

"How is it you were able to touch the case without being shocked?"

She shook her head, "I don't know. I felt pulled to this case. I think this is it. This is the wizard weapon we need to destroy Nazirdok's powers."

Her vision shifted a tenth time, and Vega prayed for the end, as her nose began to bleed the way it had the last time she'd had so many visions at once. She saw her future self, talking to Celestia.

"Is it really over?" the queen asked, "There's not going to be some missing piece later on, is there?"

"It is over," she answered, "You have completely fulfilled the prophecy I foresaw, and there will be one hundred years of uninterrupted peace."

Celestia breathed a sigh of relief, the flowy blue skirt of her gown billowing around her softly. After a pause, she said, "I asked you a question last time I was here. Will you give me an answer now?"

She smiled, "I will. Everything in this world has an opposite; light and dark, day and night, moon and sun, ground and sky, plant and animal. So, every*one* has an opposite. You were able to thwart Nazirdok because *you* were his opposite. In every possible way, you were what he wasn't, and he was what you weren't. That is why you were the only one who could defeat him. No one else's power could have stopped him. He'd gathered too much energy. When you first receive your powers, you're at your strongest. He wasn't expecting anyone to be able to defeat him, least of all you. That's why he didn't take you seriously as a threat. His arrogance was his downfall. When you were able to break through his spell and stop his ritual, he was entirely unprepared for the possibility."

"I'm Nazirdok's opposite?" she asked.

"You're his downfall and his weakness," she said, "Everything must have balance. There can only be as much good as bad in this world, and vice versa. If the scales tip too much to either side, chaos is the result."

"So, I was born to balance the darkness he created," Celestia said.

It wasn't a question, but she responded, "Yes. But, after he was defeated, and his powers contained in the orb, you became the light wizard who possesses raw power. When a wizard of one side possesses the gift, there must be a wizard of the other side who also can, for balance."

"Zandor," Celestia whispered.

Zandor? Vega thought, *Who is that? And what is "raw power?"*

"Yes," her future self replied, "Zandor is Thaandor's opposite. When his mentor was killed, he gained the ability to wield raw power, to bring balance to light and dark. You and Thaandor are the opposite pairing of Zandor and Nazirdok, in every way."

"But, if we destroyed them, doesn't that mean the balance is off again?" she asked.

She smiled, "No. You don't plan on using your powers, so there isn't a force for good that must be balanced by evil. You killed your opposites, so now you don't have them. The two of you are living against nature. Eventually, it will catch up. But, not for quite a while."

"A hundred years?" Celestia asked.

She smiled again, "Indeed. Your opposites tipped the scales toward evil, with their plan to plunge the world into darkness. You and Thaandor tipped the scales toward good, with your strong moral compasses, and your powerful magic. I only saw that one of you would win. Forces of your magnitude cannot be contained. You cannot coexist together. One of you must defeat the other. That is how I knew that your victory or failure would mean the tipping of the scales for the next hundred years."

She was silent, contemplating everything.

"No more questions?" she asked, "Normally, you're full of them."

"Normally, I'm embarking on a quest, and I need to know what to do to succeed," she said, "Now, my quest is at an end, and I only needed to know how I was able to win. So, Zandor got his powers because of me. How is it I am able to wield raw powers?"

"Your opposite was too powerful. Though Nazirdok could not wield raw power, he had massive energy stores. You had to be born with the ability to combat that."

She was silent again. After a pause, she said, "So, what now?"

"That, Celestia," her older self said, "Is up to you."

Vega came back to reality, her head exploding with pain, and blood pouring down her face from her nose. She even had a couple drops coming from her eyes. She had never known such pain before. She was having too many visions for her body to handle. Her future self had given her all the answers she needed, except for the question of who Zandor was.

As she tried to lie down to recover, another vision hit her. The man she'd seen in the first vision . . . the one who picked up the orb . . . the one who had turned into Nazirdok . . . he was Zandor! Suddenly, she blacked out, her body unable to keep going.

Her eyes fluttered open. She wasn't sure how long she'd been out. She still felt lingering pain in her head, and dried blood on her face. Tabatha was hovering over her, looking concerned. As she stared at the ivory pixie, she whispered, "I'm alright. Sorry for worrying you."

A tear streamed from her eyes, caused by the pain she was still experiencing, "I wish my visions didn't cause me such pain." She began to sob softly, but it only made her headache worse.

Pixie dust rained down upon her, and as she looked up, she realized she was being granted a pixie wish by Tabatha. The pain in her head subsided, and she felt refreshed. She sat up as the glow of pixie magic began to radiate from her own body. Pulses of wind and light moved from her in waves, just as they did from her pixie friend. She looked down, realizing she was glowing now.

"Oh, thank you, Tabatha!" she shouted, overjoyed and relieved that her pain had vanished.

The tiny pixie twirled around, happy to have helped her.

But, Vega could see she was tired from the magical exertion. She held out her hand, carrying her to her little bed so she could rest. As she watched over the sleeping pixie, she smiled. Her visions would no longer cause her pain. She felt freer than she ever had.

The next day, she worked her scheduled hours, providing answers for several paying customers Thaandor had sent her way. When she was off-duty, she spent the rest of the day mulling over the things she'd seen, and trying to make sense of everything. She wrote down all the visions she'd had related to her prophecy. She laid them out across her floor, trying to revisit each of them, and understand the complete picture of what was to happen, and how she could ensure their success.

It was a complicated web of future events, and she wasn't sure she fully understood it all. She pinned the vision pieces to the wall in her guest room, using it as a studio to map out her prophecies. She felt better once it was all on paper, like she had released it all somehow. She figured she could show it to Thaandor upon his return, and that perhaps he could help her sort it all out.

In the meantime, she planned to establish her new routine, and begin to enjoy her life again. She was cautiously optimistic, as every time she thought things were going well, something bad happened. She was almost waiting for something—expecting something to go wrong. But, for the next few months, everything was fine. She finally had everything she had ever wanted. She had a peaceful, quiet life, with a job that didn't hurt her or take her over any longer.

Thaandor returned from his travels, campaigning for her services. When she told him of what had happened, and how her visions would no longer hurt her, he was thrilled. She showed him her map of visions, asking for his wisdom.

"I shall need to take time to review them," he replied, staring at the words she had written in amazement.

She nodded, "I have certainly spent enough time processing them in my own mind. Perhaps a fresh perspective would help."

He gave her a nod of agreement, contemplating, "There is certainly a lot to process."

"Tell me about it," she smirked.

He shook his head in disbelief, "How did one so young survive such visions?"

"I don't know," she answered, "I can only tell you what I've seen. Now, I think I shall be able to survive them much more easily in the future, thanks to Tabatha."

He gave her a soft smile, "You make interesting friends wherever you go. Perhaps you should accompany me on the campaign trail next time."

"No," she said solemnly, "It's too dangerous for me on the road. Not to mention, if I'm gone, who will tend to the customers who come in our absence?"

Thaandor sighed, "I suppose you're right. Still, I'm sure your friends will miss you."

"I'll miss them, too," she replied, "Always. But, they can still visit me if they wish."

"That is if they are able," he said, "I'm sure they would want to."

Vega nodded in agreement, "Yes. I hope one day I'll see Cassie, Kamine, Jezebelle, my parents, Byun, and the Boreases. But, I know there is no guarantee of that."

"Well," he said, trying to cheer her up, "You have a long life ahead of you to find out. Perhaps at least some of them will visit you."

She gave him a weak smile, nodding doubtfully.

"Well, I'm heading home for the night," he said, "I shall see you tomorrow."

"Be ready for a full day of facilitating customers," she replied.

"Of course not," he chided, "Only until lunch." He gave her a wink as he headed out the door.

She chuckled to herself, shaking her head.

The next day was spent sharing more visions with their clientele. Thaandor happily facilitated their exchanges, handling the money, and talking her up before allowing them inside. Vega's head didn't hurt at all as she read future after future. She felt mystical in her new outfit, with wind and light radiating from her. The effect complimented her glowing white eyes that showed no pupil or iris. Now, she looked the part. No one would question whether she was The Oracle.

She saw future events, both good and bad. The more she read about oracles, the more she began to understand about herself and her abilities. She even learned how to detect and block other oracles, as Katrina had done to her. Without the painful headaches her visions used to bring, she was able to keep a clear, focused head, and expand on her abilities.

Thaandor helped her as well, studying alongside her, and sharing any useful information. He helped her learn how to focus and tune into her abilities. It was very similar to how wizards used their magic, so it was easy for him to understand and teach. He also tried to help her understand her visions.

"I have looked through your web of visions, and spent time pondering each one," he said.

Vega looked at him eagerly, "What have you come up with?"

Thaandor sighed, "Nothing new. I'm honestly amazed at how much *you* were able to decipher. I must say, I was lost. Were those *all* of your visions?"

She had left out any visions that pertained to Thaandor, not wanting to tell him anything before he was ready to hear it. So, unfortunately, they were more confusing for him than for her, because he was missing pieces. She sighed, "Not *all*. But, all the ones I am able to share."

He nodded, "Well, that makes more sense. But, I'm afraid I can be of no help to you, then."

"What is 'raw power?'" she asked.

He looked at her, "Where did you hear that?"

"Umm . . . it was in a book I was reading. It, uh, didn't explain it very well."

Thaandor eyed her suspiciously, but didn't say anything. After a pause, he said, "Remember when I taught you the spell to construct your house?"

She nodded.

"Remember how you had to tune into your current of power?"

Vega gave him another nod.

"Well, past when a wizard first gets his powers, we are unable to tap into the raw power within us. We can only access a small stream of it. But, throughout our history, there have been a small handful of wizards able to tap into their raw power, and wield it with control. They are the most powerful of us all. They have access to their bodies' greatest reserves of strength and power. I've never known one in my lifetime who could wield theirs."

She sat pondering a moment, amazed. *So, Celestia will be able to wield raw power?* she thought.

"Would you like to see some of the wizards who could wield it?" Thaandor asked, "They have displays for them at The Wizarding Museum."

Vega looked at him, "Sure. That would be wonderful. I need to still get out of the house sometimes."

He smiled, and the two of them planned a trip to the museum. It was nice, being able to go out and do things with her keeper. Though most of the time, he would be busy facilitating her exchanges or advertising her services, she was still able to see him frequently. He kept his own house, preferring to maintain some level of solitude. It wasn't too far from her own abode, and he frequently stuck around after hours to help her learn, or to just hang out. He also took care of the food shopping—providing for her and caring for her, as a good keeper should.

When he went out on the campaign trail, Vega made it clear that part of his job was to act as her liaison among the other lands and races, maintaining good relationships with them all. She also ensured her vision would come true, by encouraging Thaandor to talk to Sarafin on Kirstiana's behalf.

Time passed, and they found happiness and security in their new roles. She was no longer a little girl struggling to understand her "episodes," and trying to be a normal kid. She was a young lady, possessing the wisdom of the Tree of Knowledge and the magic of the pixies. She had a home, a keeper, a routine. She no longer had to feel like a vessel being tossed about in a stormy sea, as she blindly navigated her own life. Instead, she was a proud ship on clear waters. She no longer needed a compass. She knew where to go. And finally, that was home.

The End

18

"Aurano! Nastazya!" Celestia called. She wore a flowing blue gown, blonde hair cascading around her, with a silver tiara upon her head. Bridgot stood beside her. He wore blue royal robes with a silver crown upon his brown, curly hair.

Vega stared in wonder as two young children came running into the corridor where they were standing. The boy had curly, blonde hair and blue eyes, and the girl had brown, wispy hair and gray eyes. She was shocked, at first, that they had named their children after their two warrior friends who'd been killed. But, after a moment's thought, she wasn't really surprised at all.

"Your grandmother has a surprise for you," Celestia said.

The two kids squealed excitedly, and they followed their parents outside, where Lady Eva had set up a large track for a wooden cart. When they saw it, they screamed with delight, racing each other over to it. Aurano climbed behind the wheel, and Nastazya clambered in beside him. Their parents watched contentedly as their grandmother gave them a push, and they took off down the track.

The vision shifted, and she saw the kingdom gathered before them. Bridgot and Celestia were a bit older. So were their children. Their daughter, Nastazya had blossomed into a beauty. She looked just like her mother and grandmother, except for her wispy hair. And, of course, they each had a different hair and eye color. Eva's hair was caramel, her eyes mahogany. Celestia's hair was white-blonde, her eyes blue. Nastazya's hair was light brown, her eyes gray. She wore a gold ballgown and jewelry, with a tiara on her head.

Aurano looked just like Bridgot, except his hair and eye color, which matched Celestia's. As Vega watched, he stood before the thrones of Ivétoiless, reciting his vows to be king. Bridgot's crown was removed, and placed upon his son's head.

Then, a woman with black hair and brown eyes stepped up beside him. She wore a deep purple gown, and she smiled at Aurano. She stood tall and proud, reciting her vows to become queen. Celestia's crown was removed, and placed upon her head. Vega realized that she must be Aurano's wife.

Once the coronation ceremony had ended, Aurano squeezed her hand, saying, "We did it." He brought her hand to his lips, kissing it.

Bridgot and Celestia came over, embracing the two of them. Celestia took her arm as she said, "I've no doubt the two of you will maintain the prosperity of our kingdom. My son did well in choosing you, Ravinia. I'm proud to call you my daughter-in-law."

She blushed, "Thank you. I don't know what to say."

The vision shifted again, causing Vega no pain. Aurano and Ravinia were busily working, handling the concerns of their people. As they were, two kids ran through the room. Ravinia hurried to intercept them, leaving Aurano to handle the people.

"Kgansten, Thaandor, what have we told you two about running through the castle when mommy and daddy are working?" she scolded.

Kgansten looked like a miniature version of his father, with curly, blonde hair and blue eyes. Thaandor was the male version of his mother, with straight, black hair and brown eyes. Vega smiled to herself at the names they had given their children. Their whole family seemed very nostalgic when it came to names.

The nannies hurried into the room shortly after, dragging the two boys out so their parents could work. "We'll be done soon," Ravinia said, "Just play outside 'til we're finished. Then, I promise we'll all go horseback riding."

The vision shifted, and she was in a different castle. Nastazya was there, along with a man with brown hair and eyes. They both wore crowns, and Vega could see they were king and queen.

"Richard," Nastazya said, "Where are the kids? We should be leaving."

"The nannies are bringing them now," Richard replied.

No sooner had he said it than three children came into the room, dragging their heels for the nannies.

"There you are," Nastazya said, "Xharia, get your siblings' bags in the carriage. It's time to go." As their oldest—a little beauty with brown hair and eyes—started lugging her bags to the carriage, she turned to the other two, "Ladon, Natasha, you can carry the small bags. Come on." The two younger kids had brown hair and gray eyes, like their mother. They all began lugging bags to the carriage, preparing to set out.

"Why do you have them do it, when that's what our servants are for?" Richard asked.

"Because," she replied, "It teaches them that they are not better than their people. It teaches them to be humble, rather than arrogant."

The vision shifted again, and she could see Bridgot and Celestia, older. Their hair was graying with age. They were retired nobles.

"Celestia, remember when I said my thirst for adventure would be satisfied for a hundred years?" Bridgot asked.

She nodded.

"Well, I know it hasn't been a hundred, but it has returned. The life of a retired king is boring. I feel useless."

"I agree with you," she replied, "Our children are grown. Our grandchildren are on the throne. We even have great-grandchildren now. There is nothing left for us to do here. There is no one to advise. I always thought becoming queen was the end. I saw it as what I'd be doing the rest of my life. But now . . . now I realize that it's not. My time as queen is over. Yet, there is still life in me."

He nodded, "Exactly. We should *do* something with the rest of our lives." He paused, finally saying, "I think we should travel. The only times we've gotten to see the world, we were under extreme duress. We didn't get to *enjoy* ourselves. We didn't get to take our time."

"You're right," Celestia said, "We have nothing but time now. We *should* see the world."

Vega watched as she saw flashes of the two of them in various places. First, they journeyed to the far-off land of Tomainda, where Celestia's grandmother, Dia, was from. It brought back her vision of when Jon had brought Dia home to meet B. She met the descendants of her grandmother's sisters; Kanika, Wamuiru, and Bia.

Then, they journeyed to Kataran. It was hard for Vega to look at her old home. Yet, she knew it would be Bridgot's home, too. She saw his family. His parents had passed away, but he had many siblings. His older sister, Margaret lived with her husband, James, happily growing old together. Their children had long since grown up and moved out. His older brother, Bryan, was much the same. He and his wife, Brianne had retired, living in the small series of huts near Town Hall, where all the elders lived. Their grandchildren were running the family farm, now.

His younger sister, Kyja was even retired, along with her husband, Ethan. His younger sister, Luanne, and her husband, Dillon had recently become grandparents. Bridgot and Celestia bunked with his sister, Kyja, taking the tiny spare room of her seniors' cottage. They were happy in that village. Vega could relate. It was a place of simplicity and community.

After some time, they went to stay with the elves in Gliken. Though humans are normally not readily welcome, the two of them were. Xharia was thrilled to take them in, sharing her home with them. They wore elven robes, taking part in the customs and lifestyle of the elves. They learned all about elven culture, from their food to their creatures to their traditions. Vega thought they might have been the first and only humans to do so.

A few years passed before they journeyed to Korga, the land of the dwarves. They stayed with Kgansten and Natasha in the dwarven tunnels. Their dwarven companion had gotten very old. His hair and beard were white, his skin wrinkled. His wife was close to the same. They didn't have long left. Bridgot and Celestia had already spent ten years in the first three places they'd stayed, and Kgansten was in his nineties. He was still committed to immersing them in dwarven culture, however, full of pride for his people. They stayed with him until he died, setting out after his funeral.

Then, it was on to Cardeas, where they stayed with Nastazya's brothers. Vega hadn't yet seen them in a vision. It took her a while to find out who they were. She could see the resemblance, but she couldn't put her finger on it. It wasn't until she caught fragments of conversation that she figured it out.

"How long do you think our sister's shrine will remain in the land of the riders?"

"It will remain forever," Celestia said.

"Nastazya was a hero," Bridgot added, "Her people will honor her in their history books."

"*We* are her people," another brother said angrily, "She was Cardean before she was a rider."

"Of course," he replied, "I meant no disrespect. But you can have more than one people. I should know."

The brother sighed, "Forgive me. You are right."

When they left Cardeas, they headed to Abyumo, and the realm of the wizards. They stayed with none other than Thaandor. He worked with Celestia, training her to use her powers. They enjoyed the magic of the wizard realm. They explored The Wizarding Museum. She even caught flashes of them petting a phoenix!

Then, it was on to the realm of the dragon riders. They stayed in the castle, hosted by Kirstiana and her daughter, Lorena. They worked with the dragon caretakers, helping to look after the massive dragons. They seemed to really understand the intimidating creatures, showing no fear.

Then, she saw flashes of Bridgot getting sick. They returned to Duwazo. She saw his funeral. Finally, she saw Celestia leave again. She returned to the wizard realm, continuing to train with Thaandor. The vision shifted one last time, and she saw Thaandor's funeral. It was bittersweet, as she didn't want her keeper to die. But, at the same time, she was glad he would live to a ripe old age. Years and years had passed. She had also been sad to see Kgansten and Bridgot go, but again, she knew they had lived full, long lives.

Suddenly, she saw her future self, garbed in black, approaching Celestia, "Callisto?"

Callisto? Vega wondered, *Why would I call her Callisto?*

Celestia turned toward her. She had gray hair, silver and blue wizard robes, and a hood over her head. Her blue eyes had not dulled with age. Tears streamed from them, making them brighter. The two of them embraced, sharing their grief.

When the funeral was over, they began walking back to Vega's house.

"Callisto, I wanted to ask you something," her older self said, "I understand if you say no. I just have to ask."

Celestia brushed away her tears, "Yes?"

"Now that Thaandor's gone, I'm in need of a keeper. I'm not sure what your plans were, or whether you would want to. I know it's a hard time right now, on top of that. But, if you are willing, I'd like to ask if you would become my keeper."

She paused, considering. After a moment, she said, "I changed my name when I moved here, letting go of my old life after Bridgot died. Thaandor trained me to use my powers. He also trained me to take over for him, as he was getting older. Without that job, I have no purpose. Of course, I shall be your keeper."

As the vision faded away, Vega smiled. She was so close to her prophecy that she'd seen the entirety of its princess' life. And, it was linked with her own. Their destinies were intertwined from the moment she'd first seen her, after she met B. And, now she knew that one day, she'd be her keeper.

"Come on, Vega, get up and ready," Thaandor said, "Your customers are waiting for you." He was the keeper of The Oracle, with a long, gray beard, and brown eyes.

Vega groaned. "Five more minutes," she said, burying her face in her pillow. She was the young oracle, with golden and amber hair, and glowing white eyes.

"You've already had over an hour," he said, shaking her.

She turned over, groaning again. "Is everything ready?" she asked.

"Yes," the old wizard replied, "But, are you sure you want to do this?"

"Today's the day, Thaandor," she said confidently, "I can feel it." She shoved him from the room, dressing quickly. Once she'd gotten her turquoise oracle ensemble on, she came back out, grabbing a quick bite to eat.

He paced nervously back and forth, his light blue wizard robes trailing behind him. "I don't know," he said, "What if none of them show?"

"Well, of course, they'll show," Vega said, "You've advertised well."

He nodded uncertainly.

"Come on," she said, cleaning up, "We must get to the front room."

The two of them started heading out the door.

"Tabatha, come on!" Vega shouted.

"She's coming!" Thaandor replied.

The little, ivory pixie darted into the room, landing upon Vega's shoulder. Her curly hair was up in its bun, her ivory body glowing, her wings folded neatly against her back.

The three of them headed into Vega's front room, anxiously awaiting the wave of customers. Tabatha went to her lantern in the corner, and Vega took a seat in the middle of the floor, crossing her legs.

Thaandor went outside, preparing to facilitate customer entry. They had spent time advertising for a sale on readings. For one day only, they would be half price. They had even decided to extend their hours to the whole day for anyone who wished to come.

At first, she shared her keeper's worry that no one would show, but it didn't take long for him to send in her first customer. There was a steady stream after that, lasting the entire day. Vega was tired and hungry by the end of it, but at least she wasn't in pain. Plus, they had made over five-hundred pounds.

"I'd say that was a success," Thaandor said, as he came back inside.

"You sound surprised," Vega said, yawning.

"It was a better turn-out than expected," he replied, "Why don't I make us some food, and then you can get some rest?"

She nodded, shooting him a smile.

The two of them had breakfast for dinner, both of them hungry after working all day. Thaandor cooked up some eggs and hash browns for them, serving them with fruit and some juice. There wasn't much conversation as they shoveled it down, both of them tired and hungry.

Thaandor headed home when they'd finished, and Vega and Tabatha went to their room, curling up in their respective beds. As Vega tried to drift off, she was struck with a vision. She saw her future self again, talking with Celestia.

"One day, when the hundred years is up, your great-great-great-grandson will need your help."

"It seems so far in the future," Celestia laughed, silver hair cascading over her shoulders, "Yet, I know that it is not. It will pass in the blink of an eye from here. Just like my life."

She sighed, "His name is Orion. He is a dragon rider."

She looked at her, "Why tell me? Why now?"

"You know I tell you things only when you are meant to know them," she replied.

It was Celestia's turn to sigh, "How am I to find him, then?"

"He will come to you," she paused, "Well, he will come to me, seeking my foresight."

"So I am to accompany him, then?"

"Yes," her older self said, "You are to train him in the southern reaches of Katangalo, at the abandoned training grounds."

Celestia rolled her eyes, "Aren't I a little old for you to still be sending me on quests?"

She chuckled, "You're not even that old for a witch."

"But, I am old for a human," she retorted, "I just want to live my life in peace. I've done my share of quests."

"You have, indeed," she said, "The world is at peace thanks to you. But, he will need you. You said yourself you haven't been able to find meaning in your long life. Your first quest helped you find yourself. Your second saved your marriage. Now, you need to find yourself again. Perhaps this quest will do that."

The vision shifted, and she saw flashes of a young dragon rider with light brown skin and sapphire eyes . . . Celestia training him . . . Xharia . . . and a dwarven warrior she didn't recognize, with a black beard and terracotta skin . . .

Then, more flashes. She saw a large, dark-skinned rider with an impossibly large black dragon . . . he took over the dragon rider realm . . . death and destruction in his wake . . . taking over the rest of the world . . . his dark reign spreading over all other lands . . .

She saw Orion fighting the dark rider . . . then, she saw him shoot an arrow at Orion . . . Celestia jumping in front of him . . . dying . . .

No! she thought, *Celestia* . . .

Her keeper's body faded from view, and she saw Xharia and the brown dwarf getting married. During the celebration, Gizella said, "I heard the rider was in love with you, too. No offense, but why would you choose the dwarf? He won't live as long as you."

Xharia looked at her sadly, "I know. But I love him." She turned her gaze to the dwarf, who was dancing happily with someone Vega could only assume was his sister.

"Not to put a downer on your wedding or anything," Gizella continued, "But, why? What made you fall for a dwarf?"

She sighed, "I admire dwarves. I always have, ever since I befriended Kgansten. Their work ethic, their loyalty, their devotion. Not to mention, they live more in their short lives than most elves I've known ever do.

Mithrel is stubborn, gruff, and proud. But, he's also brave, generous, and honorable. I've seen more character from him than anyone I've ever known. And, he may be rough around the edges, but he's also tender and caring with those he loves."

Her sister looked at her, understanding.

"Orion is sweet," Xharia said, "He has heart. He's brave and determined. But, he's also young, naive, and childish at times. Orion's a boy. Mithrel's a man. I just could never see myself with a boy. I was never attracted to him. I never viewed him that way."

"But, you're attracted to a dwarf?" Gizella asked skeptically.

She shook her head, "I wouldn't expect you to understand, sis. You're a true elf, through and through. But yes, I'm attracted to Mithrel. He's strong, dark, and masculine. His skin is rough from hard work and battles, but his eyes are soft and deep."

"You really do love him," she said, "Well, I may not get it, but I'll always support you. Besides, all's well that ends well. Orion found another girl, anyway."

Xharia smiled, watching him dance with Lorena, "Yes, he did."

As Vega was marveling that Orion was with Lorena, it shifted. She saw her future self again, talking to the dark rider, "Hello, Dredon."

He grinned, towering over her, dark muscles rippling, "Hello, Oracle."

"Why have you come?"

"Don't play dumb with me," he said, "You already know."

She smiled resignedly.

"Tell me what you have foreseen," he demanded, "But, if I don't like the answer, *you* may not like what happens."

"I already know what will happen," she said, looking at him steadily, "Nothing I say will make a difference."

Dredon straightened, clearing his throat, "If you tell me how to succeed with my plan, I shall let you live. I shall make you The Oracle over my new world. You will have power, status, luxury. If you refuse, only then shall I kill you."

Kill me? Vega thought in panic.

Her future self sighed, "I've seen the ways this all plays out, lest you forget. I've seen what 'your world' looks like, and I would never want to help you achieve it. That's why, despite the danger to myself, I sent everyone I could to aid the one who can stop you."

He yelled out in anger, slapping her across the face, "Tell me what you know!"

She looked up at him, calm and steady, a thin line of blood trickling from her lip, "No." She paused, staring at him with a strength Vega never knew she could possess, "Regardless of what it means for me, I will not help you. If I am to die, I will die on the side of righteousness, not cowering under the side of darkness." With that, she spat blood at him.

Dredon's eyes darkened as he looked at her. He brushed the blood from his armor, "Very well. If death is what you wish, I shall give it to you." He summoned a curse with his magic, launching it at her.

To Vega's horror, she watched herself collapse to the ground, dead.

He lifted her body, carrying it from her house to the realm of the dragon riders.

As the vision faded, Vega let a few tears stream down. She and Celestia were both going to die at the hands of that tyrant? She was overcome with emotion, both good and bad. Bad, because they would both be killed. Yet good, because by their deaths, they would save the world. Their lives were intertwined to the very end. And, she was glad to know how brave she would become. She'd never seen herself that way before. She showed no fear at all. She didn't even flinch when he killed her.

Vega decided she wouldn't record her latest visions, preferring to keep them to herself. This was a personal battle she would have to face. She was sure more visions would come, showing her why this would have to happen, and what the results would be otherwise. But for now, she only knew she would die a hero. And, if she had to go out, she was glad she would go out doing what was right.

What now? she thought to herself. Then, her answer came to her, and she smirked. In the words of a wise woman she didn't yet have the pleasure to know, *That . . . is up to you.* A wave of raw emotion hit her as she thought that, a single tear escaping down her cheek as she smiled.

THE END

Pronunciation Guide

Characters:

Vega (veh-guh)
Thaandor (thann-door)
Boreas (bor-ee-us)
Byun (yoon)
Fughar (foo-gar)
Thrindil (thrin-dill)

Cities/Kingdoms/Villages:

Kataran (kat-uh-ran)
Garellis (guh-rell-iss)
Dirthix (der-thix)
Khanjgi (con-jee)
Kiken (kee-ken)
Cabri (kah-bree)
Ivétoiless (eve-ay-twol-ess)
Chemsson (shem-son)

Countries/Lands:

Duwazo (dew-way-zo)
Katangalo (kat-ann-gall-oh)
Gliken (glī-ken)
Korga (core-guh)
Gachichken (guh-cheech-ken)
Abyumo (ab-bee-you-moh)
Cardeas (car-dee-yes)
Fluorasti (floor-ah-stee)
Mashang (muh-shang)
Kogatsa (koh-got-suh)
Millhaymae (mill-hay-may)

Learn Dwarvish

Bie: I/me
Sie: us/we
Gyo: you
Yaug: he/she/they/them/it
Zaug: this/that/here/there
Es: is/are
Ie: and
O: or
U: on
I: from
Fu: for
Aye: yes
In: negative (no/not/nor/won't/wouldn't)
Konder: can/able/will
Frug: friend
Feinedo: foe
Brathnas: brothers

Siestras: sisters
Jdaren: thank you
Kguys: way/direction
Haill: come/originate/hail
Iskeet: seek/look/search
Yatren: trust/truth/true
Vrada: must/have to/need to
Vraden: hurt/harm
Hilgite: help/assist/accommodate
Zatrage: orders
Draigyhr: dragon
Neet: night
Jhutz: shelter/accommodations
Gnozim: room/suite/bed
On: one
Du: two

The Unsolvable Riddle

Born from ash
To ash return
But, not all of us will burn

Answer:

The elemental birds (dirthens, dwervas, auristras, phoenixes)

Explanation:

They are all born from their ashes, returning to ash when they die, but only phoenixes have the fire element.

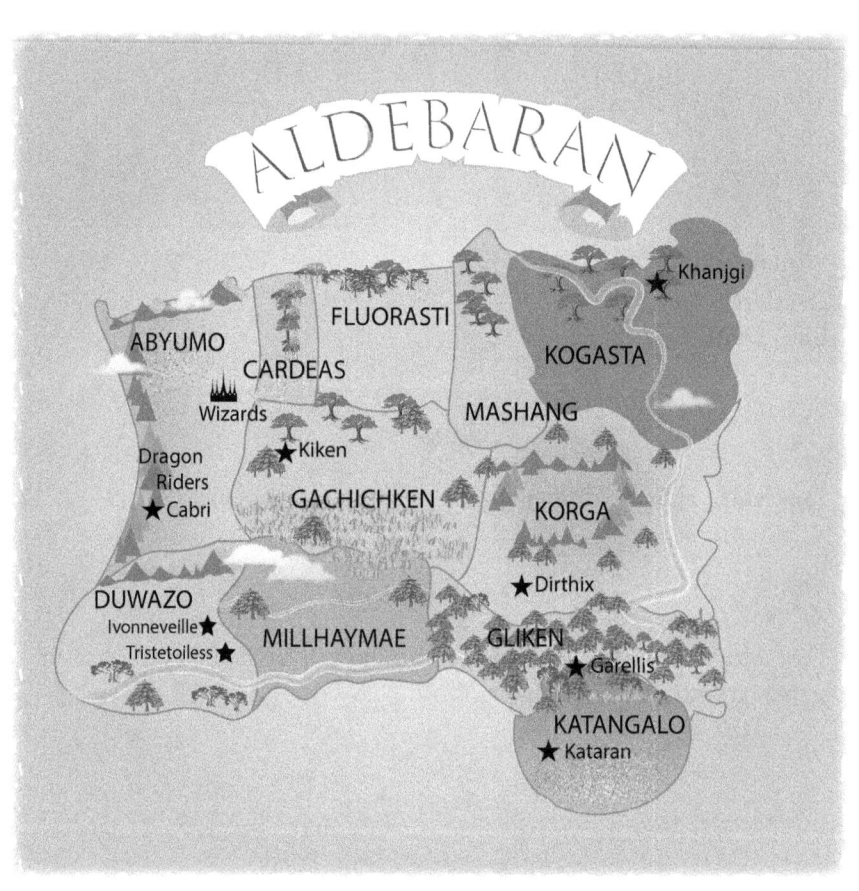

The Star Chronicles

Book 1: *When the Stars Align*

Book 2: *When the Stars Fall*

Book 3: *When the Stars Collide*

Book 4: *When the Stars Form*

www.ingramcontent.com/pod-product-compliance
Lightning Source LLC
Chambersburg PA
CBHW051527050726
47503CB00014B/2060